THE

DIVER'S CLOTHES
LIE EMPTY

"Unequivocally a thriller, but more movingly, a meditation on identity."
—*Vanity Fair*

"An emotionally precise and absorbing meditation on how grief can divest us of our most fundamental sense of self."
—*San Francisco Chronicle*

"Smart, thoroughly engrossing, funny. . . . Part mystery/thriller and part absurdist/post-modern novel with a feminist slant."
—*New York Journal of Books*

"A page-turning thriller with a subtle, satirical bent."
—*Los Angeles Times*

"Moving, clever and bright as a button."
—*The Independent* (UK)

"A literary tour de force."   —*O, The Oprah Magazine*

"A gently postmodern, surrealist philosophical novel on the protean nature of personal identity. That it manages to do this gracefully and in the span of 212 pages is remarkable."
—*Bookforum*

"The novel packs a wallop, taking the themes of Camus and Kierkegaard and transplanting them into a story with the pace and intrigue of a page-turner. . . . A speedy and suspenseful fish-out-of-water tale with a slyly philosophical bent."
—*Kirkus Reviews*

"Vendela Vida's work is utterly compelling, surprising, economical, lush, beautifully written. Reading her inspires me, and reminds me of how powerful the novel can be—how addictive and vital—and of how rarely a writer as precise, artful, and passionate as her comes along."   —George Saunders

THE

DIVER'S CLOTHES
LIE EMPTY

A Novel

VENDELA VIDA

An Imprint of HarperCollins*Publishers*

HarperCollins books may be purchased for educational, business,
or sales promotional use. For information please e-mail the Special
Markets Department at SPsales@harpercollins.com.

A hardcover edition of this book was published in 2015 by Ecco,
an imprint of HarperCollins Publishers.

FIRST ECCO PAPERBACK EDITION PUBLISHED 2016.

Designed by Suet Yee Chong

Library of Congress Cataloging-in-Publication Data has been
applied for.

ISBN 978-0-06-211094-7

16 17 18 19 20   OV/RRD   10 9 8 7 6 5 4 3 2 1

The only ones who could depart this civilization were those whose special role is to depart it: a scientist is given leave, a priest is given permission. But not a woman who doesn't even have the guarantees of a title. And I was fleeing, uneasily I was fleeing.

—Clarice Lispector, *The Passion According to G.H.*

When you find your seat you glance at the businessman sitting next to you and decide he's almost handsome. This is the second leg of your trip from Miami to Casablanca, and the distance traveled already has muted the horror of the last two months. What's to stop you from having a conversation with this man, possibly even ordering two vodka tonics with the little lemon wedges that the flight attendant will place into your plastic cups with silver tongs? He's around your age, thirty-three, and, like you, appears to be traveling alone. He has two newspapers on his lap, one in Arabic, and the other in English. If you get along well enough, you could enjoy a meal together once you get to Casablanca. You'll go to dinner and you'll sit on plush, embroidered pillows and eat couscous with your hands. Afterwards, you'll pass by the strange geometry of an unknown skyline as you make your way back to one of your hotels. Isn't this what people do when they're alone and abroad?

But as you get settled into your seat next to this businessman he tells you he plans to sleep the entire flight to Casablanca.

Then, with a considerable and embarrassing amount of effort he inflates a neck pillow with his thin lips, places a small pill on his outstretched tongue, and turns away from you and toward the oval window, the shade of which has already been shut.

As the flight takes off, the inevitable cries of babies start up and you absentmindedly flip through your guidebook to Morocco. You read: "The first thing to do upon arriving in Casablanca is get out of Casablanca." Damn. You've already booked a hotel room there for three nights. You should be annoyed with yourself for not reading the guidebook before reserving and paying for your room, but instead you direct your annoyance at the guidebook itself for telling you your first three days in Morocco will be wasted. You stuff the book deep into your backpack and remove your camera. It's a few months old, and though you've used it, you've kept it in its box with the instructions, which you have not yet read. You decide now is a good time to read them and figure out how to download the photos of your newborn niece onto your laptop. You turn the camera on—it's a Pentax, a professional camera that's nicer than you need—and study a photo of your niece on the day she was born. You feel your eyes start to well up and you turn the camera off.

The plane has still not reached a comfortable cruising altitude and the seat-belt sign has not yet been turned off, but this doesn't prevent a Western-looking woman across the aisle and two rows ahead from standing up. Wearing a dress patterned with autumnal leaves even though it's spring, she removes her carry-on suitcase from the overhead compartment. Then she sits down, places it on her lap, opens it, shifts a few items of meticulously packed clothing around to a different position within the case, closes it, and lifts the suitcase back up to the overhead compartment. A flight attendant briskly approaches and reminds her the seat-belt sign is still illuminated. The woman in the autumnal dress sits for five minutes before she is unable to control herself and stands once more to retrieve her suitcase, place it in her lap, open it, and rearrange the clothing before restoring the suitcase to the cabinet above her seat.

Your fellow passengers—half of whom look like tourists, and half like they might be Moroccans returning home—make eye contact with you and with each other and pupils are rolled. It's collectively understood that this woman is suffering from an obsessive-compulsive disorder. When the woman in the autumnal dress stands for a third time, the passenger seated in front of her, holding a book and wearing glasses, abruptly turns around to stare. She is part of a group of women who have been traveling with you since Miami. Judging by their Florida State University sweatshirts and their approximate age, you assume they attended FSU together almost forty years ago, and are on a reunion trip.

There's something familiar about this bespectacled woman who's now turned and looking back, and as you lock eyes for a moment, you sense she's maybe wondering if she recognizes you from somewhere. You spot one of this woman's sneakers, turned outward in the aisle—a clean, puffy white Reebok— and you immediately know where you last saw her. Your heart races the way it does when you've had too much caffeine. You avert your eyes from hers and concentrate on the seat back in front of you. You pull down the tray table and place your head on it. You do not want this woman to recognize you, to ask you questions.

You are careful not to peer out into the aisle again, no matter how many times the woman in the autumnal dress stands up and sits down, no matter how many times the flight attendants come down the aisle to confront her and remind her that she must remain seated. You order a glass of wine from one of these flight attendants and you take a Unisom. You know you are not supposed to mix alcohol with this tablet but you're suddenly afraid of passing the duration of the flight awake and anxious, of arriving in Casablanca feeling ragged and wrecked. You close your eyes and think of sex, which is what you think about when you have trouble sleeping. You see flashes of body parts and scenarios—some that you've seen in films, and a few you've experienced. You think of the sunscreen-smelling boy you kissed in a hammock on the beach when you were eighteen, the man from Dubrovnik who accompanied you to an Irish bar when you were twenty-five, a scene from an Italian film with Jack Nicholson and a foreign actress whose name you don't remember. You think of the girl with the green eyes at the loft party whose hand brushed over your breasts. She looked back but you didn't follow.

None of this helps: you cannot sleep. The children on the plane are screaming, especially the little girl across the aisle from you who is sitting in her mother's lap. Her hair is braided into multiple plaits, secured with bows. Usually girls in braids make you tender—they remind you of your own childhood, of how your mother came into your room every morning at six and wove your hair into two tight braids. At the ends she tied bows out of short pieces of thick fraying yarn, usually red or yellow in color to match your school uniform. She did all this while you slept because she needed to be at work before 7 A.M. Even if the strokes of her brush or the rapid motion of her fingers roused you, you were careful not to reveal you were awake. You knew she would be upset with herself that she had deprived you of sleep, so you kept your eyes shut and mimicked the slow breath of slumber.

You attended an expensive all-girls school on scholarship and not many of the other mothers worked, so she wanted to say to any mother who was watching (and they were always watching): *Yes, we are middle class, yes, I work, but my daughter isn't the worse for it—look at her neat, tight braids.* For reasons that were never clear to you at the time, your twin sister was not given a scholarship to the school and attended the public school near your apartment building. Not that you will ever pity her: she was always prettier (you are fraternal twins, not identical) and more outgoing. The result of this combination meant she was more frequently in trouble. She wore her hair cut short even when it wasn't stylish, but usually it was. You, on the other hand, had braids until you were in the seventh grade.

The girl with the braids sitting across the aisle from you in her mother's lap repeatedly startles you out of your dips into sleep with her shrieks, which are followed by her mother's attempts to quiet them. Her mother is almost louder in her soothing, as though to reassure everyone around her— *look, I'm doing my best.* You squint at her with judging eyes, though you know if you ever have children of your own you will do the same—you will soothe too loudly. One thing you observed at your all-girls school: half of parenting is a performance for others.

When the plane begins to descend into Casablanca, you organize your belongings inside your backpack. You will need to get off the plane without making contact with the FSU woman in the white puffy Reeboks. The businessman next to you wakes with five rapid blinks. He smiles at you and you smile weakly in return because you are envious of the sleep he has slept. When the plane lands, it veers left, then right, and then finds its way into a straight line. Your fellow passengers roar with applause. The cockpit door is closed, so they're not clapping for the pilots. They are clapping because their existence persists, because they are not aflame on the tarmac, because they did not disintegrate over the Atlantic. The scattered applause seems too muted a celebration of living, so you choose not to clap.

Now, as everyone stands, waiting to disembark, the children's cries are loud and the parents have given up on comforting them. When the doors to the plane open, there's a palpable, collective thrust of passengers toward the front. Everyone who has not yet stood, rises. As you gather your things—your blue suitcase and nondescript black canvas backpack that doesn't demand any attention, both of which you bought yesterday, for this trip—someone from the row behind yours tries to cut in front of you. This is the way of air travel: fellow passengers applaud because they didn't die, and then they cut in front of you so they can exit four seconds earlier.

Unlike the women on the college reunion tour, you don't

have to wait for your checked luggage, so you can pass them and progress through customs. Plans have been made for someone to pick you up, and you've been told the driver will have a sign. You see him right away, a thin man in black jeans holding a piece of yellowed paper with your name scrawled upon it. He spells your name the French way; of course he would. You studied French at your all-girls school because a Parisian heiress started the school and French was required of its students. Now as you speak this language of your youth you find yourself remembering words you didn't know you knew, and making mistakes that you immediately recognize as mistakes. You ask the driver how long it will take to get to the hotel (thirty minutes), how the weather has been (rainy), and after that there's not much to talk about. He asks where you are from and you tell him Florida and he tells you he's been to Idaho to visit relatives. You smile and say it's beautiful there. *"C'est beau là,"* you say. He agrees. You have never been to Idaho.

Outside the window of the van the sky is white, the grass green. You pass by vacant lots, billboards for cellphone companies and cars, and then the tall cream-colored buildings of Casablanca shoot up suddenly, all at once, in the distance. You see young men hitchhiking, and the driver tells you that they're trying to get to school, to college. Isn't there a bus? you ask. Yes, he says, but they don't want to wait for the bus.

The traffic is bad in Casablanca and the driver tells you it's always bad. You wish you had listened more closely when he introduced himself because now it's too late to ask him again what his name is, and you have no idea. At a stoplight, a man on a motorbike with a camouflaged-patterned trunk on the back slams into the side of the van. He was trying to get ahead in the traffic. Though you're in the middle of a road, the driver stops the van and steps out and they argue in the street. They yell and the driver gesticulates dramatically, then he gets back into the van, and you drive on with sudden, stuttering stops.

The streets seem wild to you now—so many trucks and so much smog, and the potential for motorbikes to bump against vans. The buildings around you are ugly. They once were white but now are dusted with soot. There's nothing to look at through the window except traffic. You can't wait to check into your hotel room.

You pass by an upscale Regency Hotel, an expensive-looking Sofitel, and when the driver says your hotel is close, you're happy because you think your hotel might be on par with these other tall, glassy buildings. You've been told your hotel, the Golden Tulip, is comfortable, and you've been looking forward to this comfort on the plane and in the van, but as you approach you're disappointed. The Golden Tulip has a glossy black entrance with two long banners, one advertising its restaurant and another advertising its pool. It looks like a typical tourist hotel, the kind that large groups might stay at for two nights before going to the next city on their itinerary. As the driver pulls up you see and hear American and British tourists emerging from the front door. You're deflated but what did you expect? That it would be full of locals? It's a hotel.

The driver opens the side door of the van and retrieves your suitcase from the rear. You tip him in U.S. dollars because it's all you have. You took out $300 at Miami International because you've learned from your travels to countries like Cuba and Argentina how valuable it can be to have U.S. cash. You tip the driver with a twenty-dollar bill. Later, you will wonder if this was your initial mistake.

You pass through a security portal as you enter the hotel—the kind you go through at an airport—but you keep your backpack on, and hold the handle of your suitcase. Bellboys offer to take your bags, and you tell them you can manage. Or rather: you smile and say, "No, it's okay. I'm okay."

A long black bench runs along the side of the lobby wall, but other than that there's no place to settle into—no comfortable-looking couch or chair. This lobby is not a place for lingering. You walk to the front desk, and wait behind another couple. The lobby isn't busy, so you don't understand why the two desk clerks, both in blue-gray suits, are so frazzled.

As you stand at the desk, you notice there's an ATM to your right and you decide you will get Moroccan money there later. When the couple in front of you has moved out of the way, you approach the desk. You tell the desk clerks that you have a reservation. One of the two men says your room is not ready and you argue that when you made the reservation you were guaranteed early check-in. One of the men goes into the back office—it's unclear whether he's verifying this fact or if he's avoiding you. The remaining clerk looks at his computer. "Housekeeping is there. It will be ready in five minutes."

"Five actual minutes?" you ask. Time is not how you know it, but how the country knows it.

"Five American minutes," the man behind the desk says.

He pushes a sheet of paper toward you. On the paper you're supposed to write down your passport information. The man disappears to the back office. You assume he's gone to check on the room.

You stare at the passport information form. You take your passport from your backpack. You have your new blue suitcase in front of you and you place your backpack on top of it and lean over the suitcase and the backpack and start to fill out the form. Your name, place of birth, passport number, nationality. When you're done you call out to the clerk: "I've filled out the form."

He returns to the counter and shows you a list of names on a computer printout, and says, "Which one?" Your name is halfway down the list, which you assume must be a list of people checking in, and then he crosses out your name so thoroughly, so violently, that there's no trace of it. You are given a key to the room that is now available, and you reach for the handle of your suitcase, which is still parked in front of you.

But where is your backpack?

You look on the floor. Not there.

You touch your back. You turn around, while touching your back, as though you might get a glimpse of it over your shoulder. You tell the man behind the desk you don't have your backpack. You look at the bottom edge of the desk, which does not extend to the floor. You think it might have inadvertently slid beneath. The hotel clerk looks down at the floor on his side of the desk. Nothing.

You are growing increasingly panicked—you are in Morocco and you don't have your backpack. You think of everything in it—laptop, wallet with credit cards and all the cash you took out at Miami International. A three-month-old camera. Your library book. Your toiletries. A pair of small coral earrings. As the list of inventory of lost contents increases, you forget to breathe.

You try to explain to the unhelpful hotel clerk what's going on. He suggests that one of the bellboys might have taken the backpack up to the wrong room. He talks to the young and clean-cut Moroccan bellboys. The bellboys suggest you left it in the van; they tell you the driver is still parked outside. You don't think you left it in the van because you took your passport out of the backpack at the reception desk, didn't you? Maybe you already had the passport. You are so exhausted, so frazzled that you're no longer certain of anything. Everyone else's narrative seems more likely than yours.

You follow one of the bellboys out of the hotel. People pass you on the street—this is a crowded city—but you don't register faces. A color, red, there. A yellow hijab there. When you get to the van, it's locked, so you look through the windows. Nothing on the floor of the van. Where is the driver? Maybe the driver took the backpack and came looking for you. Maybe he's looking for you in the hotel.

You run back inside the hotel. The driver has been located and is waiting for you. He says he doesn't have the backpack. He walks outside to the van with you and unlocks it and the backpack is not there. You return to the hotel. The driver, looking very worried, speaks in Arabic with the bellboys and security guards stationed at the front door.

"They say you wear the backpack when you come in," he tells you in English. Why were you trying to speak French with him? "They say they remember you had it."

You wonder for a moment why they were looking at you so closely that they recall this, but you don't have time to wonder: you're half relieved that they remember. Your exhaustion is a curtain you cannot part.

You are beckoned to the luggage room. Someone has the idea that perhaps your backpack was moved to the luggage room, where people store bags when their room isn't ready, or when they've had to check out hours before their flight. Two hotel employees stand at the entrance to the luggage room as though they're flight attendants welcoming you on board a plane. You enter and see it's a small room with shelves, stacked with a dozen dark and travel-worn suitcases. A child's car seat. No black backpack.

You exit the claustrophobic room and walk up and down the gleaming white floors of the lobby, wondering what the hell you're going to do. A man behind the check-in counter tells you not to worry—is it the same one who was purporting to help you, or his friend? You can't tell. You can't remember anything anymore. He says there are security cameras. He points above the check-in desk. "You will watch and we will see if you had the backpack when you came in. We will look and see if the bellboy took it to someone else's room. You will look and we will see," he tells you.

"Okay," you say, wondering why these cameras weren't mentioned before. Hope expands within you, as hope does. "How do I see?" you ask.

"Wait here," he says.

"Where?" you ask.

He points to exactly where you're standing.

While you wait, you watch others checking in. You want to warn them. But warn them about what? The fact that they might have left their luggage somewhere?

A young hotel employee with hunched shoulders enters the lobby and the man behind the desk says something to him. To you he says: "He will take you."

You follow this hunched man past the ATM machine and into the elevator and you descend to the basement. He leads you into a small room where a large screen covers a cinder-block wall. The screen is divided into four quadrants and you can see that, in fuzzy black and white and mostly gray, it's currently showing what's happening in four different areas of the hotel—the front desk, the black bench in the lobby, a stairwell, and a roof. In the quadrant showing what's happening at the front desk, you can see the couple that's currently checking in. The couple you wanted to warn.

"You sat here on black bench," the man says in rough English. He points to the screen that shows the black backless bench that runs along the side of the wall, perpendicular to the check-in desk.

"No," you say. "I was standing at the check-in desk." You point to the screen where the check-in desk is being shown.

"Okay," he says. He tries to click on the box but nothing happens.

He tries to type something onto the keyboard but nothing happens.

"I need password," he says.

The hunched man gets on the phone and calls someone and asks for the security password for the computer. He types the password on the keyboard and nothing happens.

He asks whoever is on the other end of the phone to repeat the password and he tries again. You hear frustration in the form of yelling coming through the receiver.

Five minutes ago, when you were in the lobby and learned of the existence of the surveillance cameras, you had great faith they would reveal which bellboy or hotel guest mistakenly took your backpack. But now your confidence plummets.

Two other men enter the small room. One of them has a beard and you guess this is the same man who was on the phone because he shouts out the password number again. His rage is evident.

Finally the hunched man succeeds and is logged on to the computer.

The bearded man who knows the password turns to you. "You were sitting on the black bench?" he asks, pointing to the image on the screen of the bench in the lobby that runs along the wall. The bench is vacant.

"No," you say, and explain that you were at the check-in desk. You stand and point again, just to make sure there's no misunderstanding.

The bearded man instructs the hunched man to play back that camera. The hunched man sits at the computer but doesn't know how to make it work. The bearded man barks something at him, but to no avail. Three more men enter. Now there are six men in the room. Not one of them knows how to play back the video.

"Excuse me," you say from the back. "I might be able to . . . May I?" It's a small room and the men part ways so you can sit at the wooden chair in front of the computer. You have no expertise in surveillance, but this does not seem as complicated as they're making it. You use the mouse to drag the curser to the camera focused on the front desk. Then you press the rewind button and you scroll back.

The video player shows a time—10 A.M.—but it's not yet that time. "What time is it?" you ask. Everyone has a different answer. It's explained that there was a time change the day before. No one has updated the time on the recording equipment.

You can't rely on the time. You continue to rewind, slowly. You stop when you see someone who looks like you but whose hair is darker, more dramatic-looking than your own and whose white shirt looks brighter. But it's you. The monochrome surveillance camera dramatizes every shade. You appear a relic of another era. A daguerreotype; a cameo in an old locket.

You rewind the video slightly further until you don't see yourself at the desk and then you press play. You and the six men in the room observe the video in silence.

You watch as you arrive through the security portal wearing the backpack and dragging the suitcase to the front desk. The bearded man points to the camera and says something to the other men in the room. You assume that he's saying, "Look, she had the backpack when she entered the hotel."

You yourself are relieved to see this: you didn't leave it in the van; it wasn't taken while going through security.

You watch yourself arguing with the unhelpful man at the front desk about your room and how it was supposed to be ready. You watch him slide the passport information form across the desk. You watch as you remove your backpack from where it hangs on both shoulders and place it on top of your suitcase, which is standing upright on its wheels in front of you. You fill out your name, place of birth, passport number, and nationality and then you return your passport to its secure place in your backpack. You push it down inside, so it can't fall out, or be taken, from the top. You call for someone from behind the desk to help you. You see your mouth move: "I've filled out the form."

At exactly this time, on the surveillance video, you notice a figure that's been sitting on the black bench in the lobby. He's a chunky man in a suit with a lanyard and a badge; he was not there when you first arrived at the hotel. He stands and takes a diagonal and deliberate path toward you. You see him stop beside you, to your right, while your head is turned toward the left as you try to get the attention of the man behind the front desk. Then you see the chunky man's fingers inch toward your stomach. His hand passes in front of you as he gently and slowly lifts the backpack straight out from where it's resting on the suitcase.

Watching the video, the men in the small cinder-block room start shouting and pointing, and one man grabs his head with both hands as though his favorite soccer player has missed a tie-breaking goal.

On the video, you watch the chunky man in the black suit stand beside you for ten seconds, as though in disbelief of what he's gotten away with. Or perhaps it's another tactic: he doesn't want to make any sudden movements. For a brief second, it looks like he's regretting what he did, and is going to return the backpack to its original position on top of your suitcase. But then, rapidly and with determination, he pulls a strap of the black backpack up over his shoulder, walks efficiently but not too quickly toward the exit of the hotel with his head up, passes by the security men and through the security portal, turns right, and is safely on the street.

You hear a sound coming from deep inside you—a strange, guttural yelp—and you stand up. The hotel security crew are all pointing at the screen and rewinding the surveillance video and exclaiming things in Arabic. Your mind is rioting now that you know for sure your backpack is gone. You see no way out of this. You want to go home. You have just arrived in Morocco and your backpack, your identity, has been stolen. Everyone has forgotten about you; they are all turned to the screen. They are getting more excited, pointing, replaying the crime—they've finally figured out how to play the video on their own. You turn so you're facing the filing cabinets in this tiny room that is a mockery of an office. You think you might cry. *Don't cry,* you tell yourself. *Don't cry.* And you know you won't. A strange adrenaline, a forceful calmness overtakes you. You have been in situations like these before and you feel this tranquillity, the green-blue of an ocean, wash over you.

You turn back around. "I need to cancel my credit cards,"

you tell the bearded man who knew the long and complicated password. He says they are calling the police, and you nod. "They will come here?" you say.

"Yes," he tells you.

"While I'm waiting, can I make some phone calls?"

The hunched man is assigned to escort you to an office on the second floor. To get there you have to go up one elevator, and walk across the lobby to another. You pass the long black leatherette bench against the wall. It's a narrow, backless bench where no one is intended to sit for long.

On the way to the other elevator that will take you to the second floor, you see the driver of the van that transported you from the airport to the hotel. He is animated and happy. "I told you backpack not in my van," he says. "I said you have backpack when you come into hotel." You see how relieved he is that he's not responsible. So happy that your backpack was stolen by someone else!

You nod and continue being escorted to the second-floor office. A plump man in a gray suit stops you. He introduces himself as the head of security at the hotel. Where was he before? Not just when the backpack was stolen, but when the six men who couldn't figure out how to access the security videos were shouting passwords at each other and you were having to show them how to click the arrow on the computer. Where was he then?

The head of security is barrel-chested and his mustache is thick. He reminds you of the man on the Monopoly board game. The banker. He seems proud to be in charge. Even more than that: he seems proud that a theft has taken place in the hotel and that he will have to talk to the police chief. "We have called the police chief and he is on his way," he tells you. He's smiling when he says this. What is wrong with him? He's beaming with excitement and pride and doesn't apologize or say he's sorry about the loss of your backpack and its contents. He just stands there smiling, and then he tells you to relax. "Go to your room and relax. We are here," he says.

"I can't relax," you tell him. "I have to cancel my credit cards."

"Just relax," he repeats. "The police chief is coming."

You ignore him and take the elevator up to the second-floor office. "He seemed really happy about the whole thing," you say to the hunched man escorting you, forgetting that his English is not good.

"You are happy?" the hunched man asks, confused.

The elevator doors open and you exit without correcting him.

You are led to a desk in an office that has a computer and a phone. Two other people are in this office, answering phones and, you realize, taking reservations. One of these men is likely the same person who told you early check-in would be no problem. You sit down in the empty swivel chair, and as the hunched man turns and leaves the office you begin searching the Internet for phone numbers to your banks. You call your credit-card company and Christy in Denver says she will help you. You don't know your credit-card number by heart, so Christy in Denver has to access it by your name and ask you a number of security questions. When she agrees that you are who you say you are, you ask about recent charges. The last thing Christy in Denver sees being charged to your credit card was a meal at the airport in Miami.

"Great," you say, and then ask: "Are you sure I should cancel it, then? If it's not being used?"

"Do you know for a fact the card was stolen and not misplaced?" Christy asks you.

"Yes," you say. "I saw them play back the surveillance camera. It was definitely stolen."

"Then you should cancel it," she says.

So you do.

You know as you hang up that you will have to call back the credit-card company and ask what their insurance policy is for stolen items, but now is not the time to do this. You are briefly overwhelmed by the amount of phone calls you already know you'll have to make in the coming weeks and months. You are certain paperwork will be involved.

You call to cancel your bank card. Vipul in India says he can assist you. First he needs you to answer security questions, which you do. Then he asks you how much money, approximately, you have in your account.

You look to your left, toward one man taking reservations, and you look to your right, toward the other man. Neither man is on the phone at the moment and so you know they are listening to your conversation. You know their English is good because you've heard them taking the reservations.

"I'm in a public place right now," you say.

"I understand," Vipul in India says, "but I need an approximate number."

You are embarrassed to say the amount aloud because

it's considerably less than someone like you, someone who is thirty-three and in a foreign country, should have in their bank account.

Finally, you whisper the amount, and Vipul in India cancels your card and tells you a new one will be issued and mailed to the Florida address they have on file for you.

"It will arrive in three to five business days," Vipul in India tells you.

"I'm in Casablanca," you tell him.

"It will be in Florida when you return," he says.

You are done with your calls, and only then does it hit you that you have no way to get money or to pay for anything. *Fuck,* you think, and imagine spending your entire time in Morocco in this shitty hotel. You sink deep in your chair. You try not to swivel.

The young, hunched man who can't use a computer enters the office. "I have good news," he says.

You blink rapidly, taking this in.

"The head of security just watched video. He knows man who took the bag. He talks with him this morning at breakfast. He stays at this hotel. He is doctor at conference we are having here."

And he hasn't checked out? Does he want to get caught? You imagine the man as a kleptomaniac who steals because he wants to be found out and diagnosed. Or else he's a psychiatrist and the theft was part of a test case.

You are relieved. Your backpack will be returned. The head of security, who disturbed you because he was good-humored and telling you to relax, is now your friend. A hero.

You regret canceling your credit cards. You wonder if you can call Christy in Denver and Vipul in India again before you meet with the head of security. They must be able to reactivate the cards within five minutes of cancellation. There must be some law, some statute about that, you think. You hope.

"He waits for you downstairs," the hunched young man says.

"Okay," you say, and let him escort you down to the lobby.

The head of security is ecstatic. The two sides of his mustache, the left and the right, are forming their own smiles.

"You watched the video? You know the man?" you say. You can hear the excitement in your own voice, which sounds like it's coming from a different person than the despondent one speaking on the phone a few minutes ago.

"Yes," he says. "If I saw him I would know him. I saw him as closely as I am seeing you right now."

"Where is he now?" you ask.

"I don't know where he is this moment. He came to me this morning and asked where he could get breakfast. He asked in English, so he's not Moroccan because why else would he ask in English?"

"So you don't know who he is?" you say, more defeated than before your hopes were raised.

"He was wearing a badge. That means he's part of a conference of doctors at this hotel right now."

"Have you checked?"

"Well, no, because they are all meeting upstairs right now and I can't just walk into the room and start accusing doctors. I have to wait until the meeting is over."

"But what if he's not part of the conference? What if he was pretending to be?"

"I saw the badge. He's part of conference," he says, this time with less certainty. You both stare at each other. You know it's only now occurring to him that the badge might have been fake. "You should go relax and rest and we will get him," he says.

"Please stop telling me to relax and rest," you tell him. This comes out sounding louder than you intend it to. You sound exactly like the kind of person who needs to relax.

"The police chief is coming soon," he says. "We will put your bags in your room."

"I only have one bag now," you say. You are reluctant to leave your suitcase anywhere, so you've been dragging it around with you.

"Oh," says the chief of security, spotting something or someone over your shoulder.

"What?" You turn to follow his startled look. "Is it him? Is it the thief?"

"No, it's the police chief," he says.

You turn. The police chief has a dark mustache and his eyes are serious. "I'm very sorry for your loss," he tells you as he shakes your hand.

You like him right away because he's apologizing and not acting like the theft of your backpack is cause for rejoicing.

The police chief assures you all forms will be ready for you when you show up at his office. You don't know why you have to go to his office when he's here now, but you're sure there's a good reason and he gives you one: "It will only take fifteen minutes when you come," he says. "All the forms will be ready."

You wonder how he knows that you don't like filling out forms, but you appreciate that he understands this about you, that he's intuitive.

"We already have policemen on the street and in the markets looking for the man."

Of course they're scouring the markets. That's the first place the thief would go. To the markets to sell the computer, the phone, the camera.

"How many policemen?" you ask.

"Seventeen," he says.

Seventeen policemen. You try not to show how impressed you are. But seventeen policemen! The police chief is a serious man. But why not eighteen policemen? Where's the eighteenth policeman?

"They are of course also looking for the property that was stolen from you."

"Thank you," you say, wondering how the seventeen men know how to look for your property when no one has asked you what was inside your backpack. They only know from the surveillance video that your backpack was black and it was full.

"It's really important to me that I get my backpack back," you say. "It has my passport and my computer."

He nods. You have the feeling he has heard this complaint before. Crime in Casablanca must be common. You have faith in this police chief, but you have little faith that in a city of three million your backpack will be returned.

Desperation comes over you—there must be a hundred tourists right now who have filed police reports in Casablanca about stolen goods. You are just another one of them. Not distinguishable in any way. You are not even staying at one of the upscale hotels, where you're sure the victims of crimes are treated with more attention.

You hear the lie coming out of your mouth before you even have time to think it through: "I'm a writer for the *New York Times*," you say. "I'm doing a travel story on Casablanca. I really don't want to have to include this."

You stare at him. He stares at you.

"The what?" he says.

"The *New York Times*," you say.

He takes out a little notebook, the same kind of small pocket notebook detectives use in movies, and he starts to write something down.

"The what? How do you spell?" He hands you his pen.

You write down the words *New York Times* in his little notebook.

"And this is a company?" he asks. "What kind?"

"It's a newspaper," you say.

He thanks you and closes the notebook.

"How likely is it," you ask, "that you will catch this man, that you will find my things?"

"I am one hundred percent confident," he says.

"Wow," you say. You don't tell him that you were putting the likelihood at more like 5 percent. "One hundred percent," you repeat.

"Yes, one hundred percent," he says.

You're impressed he didn't say 99 percent. He could have given himself some leeway.

You shake his hand good-bye enthusiastically. Only after he's left do you realize he hasn't asked you your name.

You remain standing in the lobby once again with your blue suitcase and the head of security. He asks you if you would like to sit at the restaurant and have some lunch.

"No," you say. "I'd like to go to the police station."

"Yes," he says. "Someone from the hotel will take you there in a few minutes. But the head of police wants to make sure he gets the papers ready."

"Yes," you say. You don't want to be with this man anymore. His smile is disturbing you. His mustache is disturbing you.

"Why don't you go put your suitcase in your room, and when you come back downstairs someone will take you."

"Okay," you say.

It seems like days have gone by since you were given your key card. You're almost surprised you still have it. You have to look at the room number written on the small accompanying sleeve to see what floor you're on.

You enter your dark room, and place your suitcase on the suitcase stand. The stand's straps are worn out from bearing the weight of the luggage of past travelers. Out the window you have no view except for the back of another hotel.

Before leaving your room, you move your suitcase so it's under the bed, out of sight. You can think of nowhere else to hide it.

As you walk to the elevator you pass a room-service cart that's waiting to be ushered back to the kitchen. On the top of the cart sits a basket of bread rolls of various sizes and shapes, seeded and unseeded, light and dark. You consider stashing a few of them in your purse before you remember you have no purse, no backpack. You are carrying nothing. All you have is the key card in the pocket of your skirt. You grab a seeded bun. By the time the elevator lets out onto the lobby floor, you've eaten it.

A young man in a plaid shirt and clean sneakers has been assigned and paid by the hotel to take you to the police station. You have no idea what his affiliation is with the hotel—he's not in uniform—but he has kind eyes, the green of an old leather atlas, and you trust he will get you where you need to go.

He opens the backseat of the car for you and you get in. You see, on the floor of the seat next to yours, a pair of leather shoes, and you wonder what they're doing there.

The car's clock says that it's already after 2 P.M. How did it get so late? Is that the right time or yesterday's time? You know there was a time shift. You think how odd it is that they change times in the middle of the week here, not at 2 A.M. on Sundays like back home. You try to remember which day is the day of rest here, and you consider asking the driver. But instead you look out the window at the traffic surrounding you, and when you tire of all the cars and faces and gray exhaust swirling out of mufflers, you roll up your window and stare at the shoes.

"You know Paul Bowles?" the driver says, out of nowhere.

Because you're staring at the old leather shoes, you think for a brief moment he's going to tell you that they belonged to Paul Bowles.

"Yes," you say. You know who Paul Bowles is. You devoted a paragraph or maybe even a page to him in a college essay you wrote about post–World War II bohemians. You had no prior interest in the subject, nor any sustaining interest for that matter; you signed up for the class because the professor was intriguing to you. She was a burn victim, and two-thirds of her body was scarred, but this made her more beautiful. You weren't the only one who thought this: the class was filled with young male theater majors and aspiring poets. You were the sole athlete in the class. When you met with her in her office to discuss your mediocre essay, she obsessively rubbed a potent-smelling vitamin E lotion onto her shiny red wrists, her lavender-hued elbows. She kept a large tube of the lotion on the corner of her desk, where others might place a colorful paperweight. Each time she loudly squirted the lotion onto her palm, you silently marveled at the framed photos of her swimsuit-clad children, their skin impeccably unflawed.

"Everyone knows Morocco because of Paul Bowles," the driver says. "My father read for Mr. Bowles."

"Read for him?" You are certain that Paul Bowles could read.

"At end of his life, Mr. Bowles cannot see well. My father lives in the same building and sometimes Mr. Bowles asks neighbors to read for him and so sometimes he asks my father."

"Cool," you say because you can't think of anything else appropriate.

"Yes," the driver says.

You are both silent again, watching the traffic not move.

"Is it always this bad?" you ask.

"Casablanca traffic is the very most bad in Morocco," he says.

You can't even see the road ahead of you because there are six large trucks.

"So many trucks," you say inanely.

"Yes, very many trucks," he says.

Your head is heavy and you realize you've nodded off. The clock in the car now says it's 3:06.

"I'm sorry. I fell asleep. Are we almost there?"

"Yes, five minutes," he tells you.

In twenty-five minutes he parks the car. The neighborhood has narrow sidewalks and many shops. Dozens of people are on the street, talking with friends, parking their cars. The driver carefully reads the signs and is sure to put the proper amount of money in the machine.

"Sorry. I don't have any money," you say.

He smiles grimly as though you've left him to face an impossible task alone.

The two of you walk down the crowded sidewalks. The sun is out and it's warm but you can tell this is still cold for Moroccans: many men wear leather jackets and all wear long pants. You don't see any women your age, only young girls and old women. Your generation of females is missing on the street.

"They said the station is next to the big grocery store," the driver says. You pass a large grocery store, with a number of people smoking outside, next to the display of small fruits.

"Here it is," he says.

You look at the decrepit building, the Moroccan flag waving from the top.

You enter the building and walk up two flights of stairs. You pass a man and a woman carrying a stroller with no child. You try not to wonder or stare. You and the man in the plaid shirt peek into a room and you see shelves of old shoe boxes, one labeled *A-Be,* the next: *Be-De.* This continues all the way through the alphabet. A child's version of a filing system.

The driver exchanges a few sentences with the policeman sitting behind the desk in the room with the shoe boxes. The driver seems upset.

"What is it?" you ask.

"This is the wrong station," he says.

"What? How did that happen?"

"The hotel told me it was the police station next to the big supermarket."

"We saw the supermarket," you say.

"Yes, but there is another police station next to a big supermarket. That's where the police chief is waiting for you."

You return to the car. The only good news about this is maybe the other police station is better organized. Maybe it doesn't use shoe boxes for filing its claims.

You drive through stifling Casablanca traffic. You nod off again. When you arrive at the other police station near the big supermarket you are told it's after 5 P.M. and the police chief has gone home for the day.

You ask if you can report the theft to someone else. You don't want another night to pass.

You are told that that's not possible; the police chief is personally handling your case.

The driver returns you to the Golden Tulip. In your room you are somewhat surprised to find your suitcase still under your bed. You change into your pajamas and order room service. When the man from room service knocks at the door, you don't open it. Instead you instruct him to leave the tray on the other side of the door.

The chicken is an entire carcass. You eat a few bites and put the tray out of sight and crawl under the floral bedspread. It reminds you of staying at your grandmother's house—you would stay with her without your sister once a week, on Fridays—in her guest room with its cumbersome bedspread. It took so much effort to make the bed on Saturday mornings. You would fold the bedspread down before placing your pillow on top of the crease, pull the bedspread over the pillow, and tuck the ends down toward the headboard. The grandmothers of your friends didn't work, had never worked, but your grandmother worked as a cashier at a department store. You visited your grandmother at the high-end store and watched her in the back office efficiently counting dollars and expertly entering coins into small paper tubes that expanded from flat to round. When she put you to bed on the nights you spent at her house, her fingers smelled of dirty metal. Placed purposefully around her small home were expensive items she only owned because the store gave her credit every Christmas in lieu of a bonus. She usually selected bowls of orange glass, or porcelain ducks, which disappointed you. The store she worked at sold so many brighter, shinier objects, slathered in gold.

In your hotel room at the Grand Tulip you watch TV— reruns of American shows you've never seen—and try to sleep. You turn off the lights and stare into the darkness.

You wake up. You had been dreaming of the surveillance camera. Your dreams are usually in color—or so you think—but this dream was distinctly in black and white. In your dream the surveillance tape is backed up to earlier in the morning, 8 A.M.—before you arrived—and the hotel staff is talking with the man with the badge who robbed you. You wake not in a sweat but rather in full composure and clarity: the staff at the Golden Tulip was in on it.

You were set up. How did you not realize this before? Of course it was noted that you overtipped with a U.S. twenty-dollar bill. Of course your room at the Golden Tulip wasn't ready. Of course you were not attended to. Of course the desk clerks were distracted, otherwise occupied. Of course no one knew how to operate the security cameras. Of course the head of security seemed peculiarly thrilled.

But you don't blame the head of security. His behavior was so strange it suggests he was not in on the plot. He was just excited to have a security issue on his hands. His position was most likely on the chopping block, but now that a theft occurred at the hotel, he is ecstatic: he has a reason to be there. He couldn't care less about the retrieval of your bag.

The clerks at the hotel only care about not being implicated in the crime, which you are now sure they participated in. You don't know what to do with this information. Should you tell the police? Were the police in on it? Why were you taken to the wrong police station? You're not yet sure whether you will tell the police chief your suspicions. You are in a country not your own, and you have to be careful. Could the conspiracy go all the way to the top? You get a brief mental picture of the police chief enjoying your camera and phone. You imagine him taking a photo of himself in swim trunks, holding a fish he's caught without a net.

One thing you know for certain: you need to get out of this hotel. You are a target here. They got away with the theft and are now emboldened. You are scared of what will happen next here. You rise from the bed and make sure the hotel room door is locked and bolted. You turn the bathroom light on. You go to the window to make sure there's no possibility of anyone climbing in. You wonder what you'll do if someone does come in; you can't call the front desk. What is the number for the police station? In the desk drawer you find a phonebook for Casablanca. It's in Arabic and of no use to you.

You think of the gleaming, grand-looking hotels you passed when coming to the Golden Tulip. The Sofitel. The Regency.

You wait for morning to arrive. You cannot sleep. Silence takes on its own sound.

At 6:30 A.M., you call the Sofitel and ask if they have a room for tonight. You are told they are booked because of Jazzablanca. You say thank you, as though you know what Jazzablanca is.

You call the Regency and ask if they have a room for the night. Yes, they say.

"Do you have a room for a week?"

"How many people?" they ask.

"Just me. Just one," you say.

They have a room.

The woman on the phone takes your name and then tells you she needs your credit card to secure the reservation.

"I'll have to call you back with that," you say.

She goes over a few more details about the hotel and says that your passport and credit card will have to be shown at check-in.

"Of course," you say, and hang up.

You know the reservation will be canceled. You have no credit card or passport.

You think of who you could call back in America but it's the middle of the night there. You don't call your father because he's busy with his new wife and their three small sons, and you don't call your mother who now lives in Arizona, because you've chosen not to tell her about the theft. Your mother was recently fitted with a pacemaker and she waited five months to tell you this. You were strong when she told you, but that night you sobbed. You haven't told your parents about what happened before your departure, why you and your husband are divorcing.

At nine in the morning the same driver comes to meet you in the lobby. Yesterday he wore a plaid shirt and white sneakers but today he's wearing plaid sneakers and a white shirt.

In the car Paul Bowles's shoes are gone. The backseat

feels lonely, but the traffic is better today. You pass by the Regency and stare at it longingly. If only you could stay there one night; if you could feel safe enough to get a good night's sleep you know you will be able to think clearly about what to do. You will be able to make a plan. There's a part of your brain that you cannot access, that you're not rested enough to get to.

You arrive at the police station within half an hour of leaving the hotel. Again, the driver uses the machine to carefully pay for the parking ticket, and then returns to the car to place the ticket on the car's dashboard. Again, you apologize for not having any money.

You pass a sign in the lobby that is in Arabic, French, and English. The sign says POLICE STATION, NEXT FLOOR. The sign has been laminated—this is encouraging. But when you get to the top floor you panic: Has this been a ruse? The hallway is filled with mismatched chairs, all facing different directions. The police station looks like it's just been moved into, or is about to be vacated.

The plaid-sneakered man whose father once read to Paul Bowles talks to another man with a mustache and you hold your breath. This man's mustache is thin and it appears a small comb has been used to coerce the hairs to point in the same downward direction. You are convinced you'll be led back downstairs and to another police station across town.

But the mustached man nods, as though they're expecting you. The driver looks relieved. He tells you he's going outside to have a cigarette. You can smell that other people on the floor are smoking inside, so you know it's just an excuse to take a break. Maybe he wants to check on the status of his parking meter. The mustached man leads you into a room with four desks, one of which has a computer. Two other men, also with mustaches, enter the room.

You are ushered to a chair on the other side of the desk with the computer. On the desk is a box holding paper clips and erasers and thumbtacks. On the side of the box there's a calendar; the calendar is three years old. The ceilings are high and the eggshell paint on the walls is peeling. The room has a photo of a man who you assume is the King of Morocco. On top of a beige filing cabinet sits a bouquet of fake flowers. You imagine the flowers were brought in by a secretary or one of the detectives' wives who wanted to add some color, some semblance of cheer to the empty room. At some point somebody must have decided they didn't like the flowers—too pink, too prissy—so the vase was relocated to that spot above the file cabinet where you imagine they'll remain for eternity.

One of the detectives is seated at the computer and the two others sit atop bare desks. They sit like detectives.

"We are all here to listen to details of crime," one detective tells you. "We saw video. We saw what thief looks like. We do not think he was part of the conference. We think his badge was . . ."

He can't find the word.

"Fake," you suggest. You notice there's an echo in the room.

"Yes. You are not surprised?"

"No," you say. You are not surprised.

"We also see from video he has two people he works with.

They both have badges too. One outside the hotel, the other also in the lobby."

"There were three people?"

"Yes."

This makes you feel better. You were the target of a crime ring. There was probably little you could have done differently. They had fabricated badges and were going to rob someone, so they robbed you.

"Do they do this at other hotels? Make badges and rob people?"

"No, we have not heard of this before," another detective says. "It is first time."

"Oh," you say. You're not sure you believe this.

"We will start with entering information," says the man at the computer.

"Okay."

"What was your grandfather's name?"

"My grandfather?"

"Yes, it is a formality here. We have to fill out the forms."

"Anthony," you say. You have not thought of your grandfather in years. He died when you were five, and he was not such a good man. The last time you and your sister saw him you stood in front of his reclining chair, dressed in matching blue jumpers, patterned with Raggedy Ann dolls, and holding your parents' hands. Only years later did you realize you were all there to say good-bye.

Now you are giving his name to a Moroccan detective. It takes the detective five minutes to type the name. The computer or the keyboard—maybe both—are giving him trouble.

"What is your father's name?"

"Gian-Carlo," you say.

He spends five minutes typing it. He has difficulty first with "Gian," then with the hyphen, and then with "Carlo."

"Listen," you say, "I'm wondering if we can get to the part where I tell you what was stolen? I'm afraid I'll never get my computer back . . . I've already lost a day."

"You lost a die?" one of the detectives asks. "What is a die?"

"No, I lost a day. It's an expression," you say. "Don't worry about it."

"Was it a Dell?" another detective asks.

"No, a day."

"The computer was not a Dell?"

"Oh, a Dell computer!" you say.

"So it was a Dell."

"No, it was an Apple."

The three men look at you blankly. "An Apple Macintosh?" you say, slowly.

The phone rings and the detective at the desk stares at it, startled.

He says a few words into the receiver, glances at you, and is off the phone in twenty seconds.

"It's the police chief," he says. "He wants you to come to his office. He has development."

You are directed across the hall where a door is open.

The police chief beckons you in and asks you to close the door behind you. In contrast to the three detectives who were thin and nervous-seeming, the police chief seems even larger

than he was yesterday, and his office could not be more different from the spare, beige room you just left. A plush burgundy
rug expands to the edges of the room, and a blown-up map
of Casablanca takes up one wall. The curtains are burgundy
as well and cascade to the ground in thick folds. There's the
same photo of the King of Morocco, but this one is framed in
ornate gold.

From a coatrack in the corner hang two dry-cleaned suits
and at least three shirts, all in plastic bags. A tie that's already
been tied hangs from a hook.

"We have found a black backpack," the police chief says.

"That's fantastic," you say. You are stunned. You were
wrong to question him when he was 100 percent confident it
would be retrieved. This man radiates competence.

"Not everything is in it, but it has a passport and a wallet
with credit cards. Thieves here are never interested in credit
cards."

You wish you had known this before you canceled all of
yours.

He produces a black backpack from behind the desk where
he's sitting. It's not your backpack. You know it's not your
backpack but you don't have time to say anything because
he's already unzipping it and pulling out a dark blue American
passport. With a snap of his wrist, he places the passport on
the desk before you, as though he's a blackjack dealer giving
you your last card.

"I imagine everything will be easier if you have this," he
says.

You open the front page of the passport and see that while

the photo resembles you—the woman has brown straight hair and bright wide-set eyes—it is not your passport. It belongs, you see, to a woman named Sabine Alyse.

The chief of police places a red wallet in front of you.

"They took the cash from the wallet but it still has the credit cards." You wonder if these credit cards, like yours, have been canceled. You imagine using these cards to check in to the Regency and ordering everything on the menu before sleeping all the sleep you have not slept.

It strikes you as relevant that the police chief has not asked you for your name, that he has been careful with how he describes the backpack, wallet, and passport. *Here is* the *backpack, here is* the *wallet, here is* the *passport.* Not once as he called any of them yours.

You stare at the coatrack, at the expensive-looking tie that's already tied. Shaped like a noose. You do not have many options. You know this. The police chief is suggesting you claim something that isn't yours. And you're not sure what will happen if you protest. You stare at the map of Casablanca on the wall. The city is large and overwhelming, its many rectangular piers jutting out from the rest of the city like large teeth.

You now know you will take the backpack and the passport and the wallet and check in to the Regency. Once you're in the Regency you will feel safe. You need to feel safe to sleep. Once you've slept you will go to the American embassy and tell them it was a mistake, that the police returned the wrong bag to you. That is the plan.

For now, you need to get out of this police station. You

need to get out of the Golden Tulip. You will not tell the police or the Golden Tulip where you're going.

You glance down under the desk and see that the chief's
shoes are to the right of where he's sitting. He's taken them off
while talking to you. He's become more comfortable; you've
grown more tense.

"So everything is finished," he says.

You consider bringing up the fact that your computer and
many other belongings are still missing. But the words he
uttered—"So everything is finished"—was a statement, not
a question.

"Yes," you say.

"Good," he says. "Then you can put that in your article.
How good the police are here in Casablanca," he says.

"Yes," you say. You'd almost forgotten about your *New
York Times* lie.

"I just need you to sign a document here saying that a
backpack was returned to you along with a wallet and a passport."

"Okay," you say.

He slides a form across the desk and hands you a pen. On
the form you sign the name you saw in the passport.

You sign "Sabine Alyse."

The chief of police doesn't look at the passport to compare
the signatures.

"I do need one thing, though," he says.

You panic. This is when he'll arrest you for pretending to
be someone else, for claiming someone else's belongings.

"I need to get this paper stamped."

Before standing, he shifts strangely in his seat. He's slipping his shoes back on beneath the desk. Then he gets up and leaves the room.

You stare at the closed passport. You don't open it. You glance around the room once again, and study the King of Morocco's eyes. It's taking the police chief a long time. What is he doing? You tell yourself that when he returns you'll say it was a misunderstanding. You don't know why you acted as if someone else's backpack and passport and wallet belong to you. You'll explain that you haven't slept in days.

The door opens and he comes in with the paper you've signed with Sabine's name. It now bears a large bloodred stamp. A circle with Arabic words in its center.

"Here's your paper," he says. "Your proof."

Finally something is yours. You put the paper in the black backpack and zip it closed. The police chief extends his hand, and you take it. He shakes it firmly and with meaning: you understand he is communicating that a deal has been made and you are to uphold your end of it. You feel a wart on the side of his thumb press into the side of your own thumb. After what seems like a full minute, he releases your hand. You walk down the stairs of the police station nervously, your shoes loud on the stone steps.

Outside, the driver is checking the dashboard of the car to see if he got a ticket. You run toward him as though he's a lost friend.

"Let's go," you say.

"You got your backpack!" he says. He looks surprised. "So we go back to the hotel?"

"Yes," you say, and your mood dampens.

You place the backpack beside you on the backseat and unzip it carefully as though worried about disturbing its contents.

You open the U.S. passport and take a better look at Sabine Alyse. To be more convincing you could cut your hair. You notice her smooth complexion. You had acne as a teenager and it left raked lines across your cheeks and chin.

You flip through the passport, taking note of the countries Sabine has been to: Switzerland, Germany, Norway, Japan, and now Morocco. Until recently she has traveled only to countries that operate with the precision of expensive electronics.

You look through her wallet: Blue Cross insurance card suggesting she has a job, AAA insurance card meaning she owns a car, store credit at J.Crew that gives you an idea of the way she must dress. Crisply. Cleanly. Never too daring or dark.

Next you pull out her notebook, a red Moleskine. On the first page is a line where the owner is asked to write their name, and another line where the owner is asked to state the reward for finding the notebook in the event that it's lost. The reward Sabine has indicated is "Happiness."

You flip to a random entry, dated a month before. You see the words "I tried to tell them it wasn't dangerous."

You close the journal. You have already done this girl enough harm by claiming her things. Reading her diary makes it worse.

"Everything is okay? Everything is returned to you?" the driver asks. His voice startles you. You had almost forgotten he was there, that you were in his car.

"Not everything," you say.

This quiets him.

"I need to stop at a shop soon," you say. You know that before you check into the Regency you will have to confirm that Sabine Alyse's credit cards work, you will need to find out whether they've been canceled.

"What kind of shop?" the driver asks.

You are at a stop sign and out your window you see a narrow store with a pyramid of body lotion on display in the window.

"This one is good," you say. He pulls over on the next block.

"If okay with you," he says, "I wait in car so we don't get ticket."

The short, older gentleman who runs the shop ignores you when you enter. He continues talking to his friends, also older men, also short. You are still without toiletries. You pick out a toothbrush, toothpaste, a hairbrush, face wash, and a pair of scissors. Would you really cut your hair to look like Sabine Alyse?

You bring everything to the glass counter. Through the top of the counter you see makeup below. The lipsticks and blushes are displayed on a deep blue velvet material, the way a fine jeweler might showcase rubies or emeralds.

The shopkeeper's friends leave, and he finally turns his attention to you. His smile is kind, sudden, as though he's an old acquaintance.

"Welcome! I have perfect makeup," he says, looking into your eyes.

Since you were a teenager and developed your first bout of acne, makeup consultants at Nordstrom's and MAC have bestowed advice on you. "Bring attention to your eyes and away from your skin," they've instructed as they rainbow eye shadow across your lids. "Bring attention to your mouth with a bright color," they've told you, swiping alarming red over your lips.

Distract, distract, distract is everyone's advice.

But this shopkeeper, wearing a green sweater vest, tells you he has the perfect makeup for you, and because he's not looking worriedly and disapprovingly and judgmentally at your skin, you trust him.

"Let me show you," he says. "May I?"

Yes, you nod.

He applies a thin layer of foundation. "You want it thin," he says. "No powder."

"You're right," you say. "Everyone always wants to do powder and that accentuates it."

"Too fast," he says. "I don't understand. Can you say again, please?"

"Good," you say. "You are right."

He applies a makeup brush over your face and you close your eyes.

"Look," he says, and you open your eyes. He's holding a handheld mirror up to your face, and you have no choice but to look. There's still the palimpsest of acne, but for the first time in fifteen years, your skin looks almost smooth.

"Can I take this to the window?" you say, carrying the mirror toward natural light.

You have consulted a number of unhelpful dermatologists over the years and have discovered a secret from a portly shopkeeper in Casablanca who looks into your eyes instead of frowning at your skin. You tell him you'd like to buy a bottle of the foundation, and then tell him you'll buy four. And two brushes. You want the magic to continue. You hope the credit card works.

The man tallies up your purchases by hand on graph paper and gives you a discount for each item. You hand him one of Sabine's credit cards and you wait. You are suddenly convinced it will not go through. It's taking a long time. But then the man at the beauty store tears off the receipt and hands you a pen. "Please sign."

You smile so broadly your face almost hurts. He sees your pleasure and hands you his business card and requests that you tell your friends about his store. Yes, of course, you say, you'll tell your friends when you get back to the U.S. the address of a narrow and nondescript beauty shop in Casablanca that sold you toiletries at a discount and charged a credit card that was not yours.

You return to the car and maybe it's your imagination, but once you're on the road again, the driver continues to sneak looks at you in his rearview mirror. He notices something is different.

The driver takes you back to the Golden Tulip and you thank him. You tell him you wish you could tip him, and he too looks dismayed that this is not an option. You flee the car quickly, wanting to escape his disappointment. You go to your room, which has still not been made up—the bedspread is contorted into an unwieldy bundle at the foot of the mattress—and pack up your things.

You take out the scissors you purchased at the beauty store and cut your long brown hair to shoulder length, like Sabine's. You place all the hair you've cut onto a long piece of toilet paper that you've stretched across the sink counter. When you're done you roll up the tissue with the hair inside and flush it down the toilet. You flush again.

You leave your key card on top of the television set. You walk through the lobby without informing anyone you're checking out, without looking in the direction of the clerks at the desk. You exit through the front door with your luggage, and the black backpack over your shoulder, and turn right.

Something about this seems familiar to you. You remember that this is exactly what the thief did when he left the Golden Tulip. He pulled the backpack onto one shoulder, exited the front door, and turned right.

You walk down the boulevard, called Place des Nations Unies, dragging your suitcase, and you immediately sense your error. There are no other Western women walking down the street alone. You keep your eyes on the Regency in the distance and you move quickly through the crowds. The sun is high in the sky and it's hot on your skin and too many faces are turning toward you. You half expect to see someone wearing your backpack.

When you arrive at the Regency, a doorman in a suit opens the door for you, greets you with "good afternoon," and then stares out at the distance to see how you've arrived—by limo or van? You are pulling your suitcase and wearing Sabine's black backpack and you realize that you're probably the only person who's arrived at the hotel by foot. You pass through a security portal and enter an enormous lobby. Its sofas are mocha colored and deep and plush. The kind of sofas that are easy to relax into, and difficult to rise from. White orchids are staged artfully throughout the lobby and Lauryn Hill music pulses softly through the speakers. Everyone is dressed as though going to a business meeting in London or an upscale lunch in New York. No one is dressed as though they are in Morocco—they are not dressed in long skirts and scarves and sandals, the clothes you imagined yourself wearing here.

To your left is the reception desk. The area in front of the desk is large and vacant and there is nowhere to sit. A theft would not happen here because there's no place for a thief to linger, to watch. Two women stand behind the desk, available for anyone who might want to check in. No women worked behind the desk at the Golden Tulip.

You approach the kinder-looking of the two women, the one with long hair who smiles with her eyes, and tell her you don't have a reservation but you called this morning and understand there's room at the hotel. She studies the computer and confirms this. You give her Sabine Alyse's passport and her credit card.

"I may want to use a different credit card eventually," you say. "So I can get frequent flier miles . . ." You congratulate yourself on giving a valid explanation. "Is it okay if I switch credit cards when I check out?"

She says that's fine. She barely glances at the passport, but slides a form across the desk. You open Sabine Alyse's passport and scribble down the relevant information.

You are asked if you would like help with your luggage and you decline politely.

As you wait for the elevator to descend from the tenth floor, you watch the numbers decrease 3-2-1, like a countdown to your fate. The elevator doors slide open smoothly like stage curtains and a young woman emerges. You do a double take because there's something familiar about her. She looks at you too. Is it Sabine? Is that why she's staring at you? Should you run away or approach her and say you've been looking for her to return something she's lost? But it's not Sabine.

You enter the elevator and study the woman's profile as she walks across the lobby. You both have olive skin (but of course her complexion is better; everyone's complexion is better) and dark brown hair. Her hair is longer than yours—it's the length of hair you had before you cut it this past hour. You're both around the same height and build, though she's younger and her stomach is flatter. In America, you probably wouldn't notice the resemblance, but here you do.

Your room is mostly white, with fluffed pillows and a light down comforter and white bathrobes and towels all awaiting you. You sit on the bed, you sit in the desk chair and swivel around. The view out the window is of the main square below. People are traversing the square and a band shell has been set up. It's vacant now and you don't know if the concert has already happened or if preparations are being made.

There are two bathrooms in your hotel room—one with just a toilet, far from the bedroom, and one with a bathtub and shower and sink. The light in the bathroom must be flattering because you don't look like you haven't slept for days and you

have been robbed of almost every possession you care about
and have spent the morning at the Casablanca police station.

Your face is thinner than when you left Florida, as though
you've lost a pound or two since taking flight. As soon as you
see this, you are ravenous. Hunger takes over you suddenly
and completely, like fear. You scan the menu and decide on an
omelet. You call room service and they greet you with "Good
afternoon, Ms. Alyse." You consider ordering in French but
decide you have been through enough challenges for one day.
You order your food. You wait. You lie on the bed for a moment. You are so tired but you are so hungry and you cannot
sleep until you have food.

You awake to knocking. You look at the pillow. You have
been drooling. You look at the clock. You have been passed
out for precisely six minutes.

You open the door and you're touched to see a flower on
the room-service tray. You know all room-service trays at
this hotel must come with a small vase with a single white
rose, but you still wish to believe that someone has sent it just
for you. When you sign the bill, charging it to the room, you
write in an extravagant tip for the gentleman who brought you
the food and the rose.

As soon as the door closes your fork hits the plate. The
omelet is delicious. Cheese and mushrooms—you ordered
only food that would be well cooked and you believed would
not make you ill. You had visited a travel clinic before your
trip to Morocco to get hepatitis and typhoid shots, and while
there you also purchased loperamide in the event of stomach
issues. But these items were in your black backpack, so now

you can't take any risks. You had never prepared for a trip as well as you had for this one—you even bought gum, a travel-size toothbrush and toothpaste kit, a small bottle of hand lotion, wet wipes, and an orange luggage tag for your new blue suitcase. You used a black permanent marker and neatly filled out the luggage tag with your name and address, and secured it onto the handle. As you were exiting the plane after everyone was clapping—was that only yesterday morning?—the new orange luggage tag fell from your suitcase. The man behind you handed it to you and you thanked him and stuffed it in the small pocket of your new black backpack. Now you own nothing with your name on it.

You have to force yourself to slow down as you tear off pieces from the baguette that accompanied your omelet, which has already disappeared.

Soon you are so full, so good; you lie down on the bed. But the moment you do you are fully alert, your toes pointed. You tell yourself you are exhausted and need to sleep. You tell yourself that if you're not asleep in ten minutes you can get up.

When you wake you see it's 3:14 P.M. You've been asleep two hours. Now, with your mind rested, the reality of what you've done settles in: you've taken someone else's credit card and passport. You have shaken hands firmly with the police chief, accepting his not-above-the-table offer.

What have you done? This is a major crime. This is a State Department issue. What will they do to you?

You need to get to the embassy. You will explain. You were afraid of not taking what the police were offering you; it was of paramount importance that you get out of the Golden

Tulip, that the hotel and the police might have been in on the scheme together. Your life was in danger.

The embassy will forgive you. You're sure everyone there will forgive you.

You shower and douse yourself with the small bottles of shampoo and conditioner and soap provided by the hotel. The fragrance is strong, herbal, unisex. As you towel off you notice that you smell like someone else, and it's not entirely unpleasant. You take note of the two white bathrobes hanging on either side of the bathtub. Their belts are tied loosely around their midsections as though a very thin person is inside each of them. You carry one bathrobe to the closet and hang it where you won't have to see it.

You dress in the most presentable outfit you have packed, a pleated skirt and a silk blouse and a light scarf. It's a combination you've never worn before. You bought the skirt because you wanted something demure for your trip, something you could imagine wearing when touring mosques.

The document from the police chief is lying flat on the desk. You will need to show the document to the embassy. You need proof that the police gave you Sabine Alyse's passport and credit card, that you didn't steal them. The document is everything. You can't lose it. In fact, you should make copies. You will go to the business center and make copies.

In the lobby you ask the long-haired woman who checked you in where the business center is, and she points you down a corridor to her left. You pass a currency-exchange booth, where another woman is working behind glass. The existence of the currency-exchange booth reminds you that you have no money, and no ability to access cash. You only have a credit card and no pin number.

You enter the business center and find the copier. The copier requires a prepaid card, so you return to the long-haired woman at reception.

You tell her you would like to use the copier and she asks how many copies you'd like to make and you tell her two. She casually hands you a card that allows you to use the Xerox machine. "Is it okay if I charge the copies to your room?" she asks.

"That's fine," you say casually, with the air of someone who has a choice.

You make your way back to the business center, again passing the currency-exchange booth, where the woman working behind the glass is now licking her fingers, counting money, as though to taunt you. An hour ago it was food that you desired, food that made you greedy; now it is the sight of money that makes you want a lot of it. You avert your gaze.

Inside the business center, you place the document the police chief gave you in the Xerox machine and make one copy to test it before making more. The paper that comes out is blank; you didn't place the original facedown. You take the blank piece of paper that the copier slides out of the machine (not unlike the way money slides out of an ATM, you can't help noticing) and fold it and place it in the pocket of your pleated skirt. You want to hide your mistake from . . . whom? You start over. You place the police document facedown on the machine, which emits a strange, stovelike smell.

The door to the business center is thrown open, and startles you. It's a businessman, probably in his thirties. Maybe French.

"Excusez-moi," he says.

"It's okay," you say. He sits down at a computer station and places his cell phone beside him. It's the latest incarnation of the iPhone, and almost instantaneously it starts to ring. The man glances at who's calling. A woman's face appears on the phone. She's holding a child. You can see this much from your vantage point. The ring is a techno beat you've heard on radio stations you pass over while driving, the kind of thing played at a disco at three in the morning. But instead of answering the phone, or turning it off, he lets it ring until the call goes to voice mail.

A second later the ringing starts again, and the iPhone flashes the same photo of the woman with child. Again, the Frenchman takes a look at his phone, ignores the call, and without turning off the ringer, returns his attention to the computer.

The sound is driving you mad. The business center is the size of a small bathroom and the phone must be set on the highest volume. You're tempted to grab the phone, answer the call, and tell the woman calling, the woman who is most likely his wife and the mother of his child, that her husband is calmly ignoring her urgent calls.

You exit the business center feeling brittle and claustrophobic and you return to the lobby. Through the glass doors at the front of the hotel you see a mass of people in black, bathed in bright lights and surrounded by complicated-looking machines. If you were anywhere but a hotel in Casablanca you would think a movie was being filmed. You walk closer. You see cameras and trolleys. A movie is being filmed. You stop and stare for a moment, and while standing, squinting, you're approached by a man in an expensive-looking suit who introduces himself as the manager of the hotel. He welcomes you to the hotel and asks your name.

"Sabine Alyse," you say. You are proud of your lack of hesitation. You haven't slept much in thirty hours, fifty hours—you're too tired to do the math and you know that doing the math will make you more tired. But you've remembered your new fake name.

"I am so very sorry for the disturbance," the manager says. You are momentarily taken aback—is he apologizing for what happened at the other hotel, the Golden Tulip?

He continues. "They are shooting a film here in front of the hotel. It's a Moroccan film company, very respected, but we did not anticipate . . ."

He searches for the words. You have no idea what he's about to say. You stare at his mouth.

"We did not know that the film crew would be dressed so shay-billy."

"Shay-billy?" you say.

"Yes, with their pants hanging down on their hips and their hair not combed . . ."

"Oh, shabbily," you say. "They're dressed shabbily."

You are merely repeating what he said, and correcting the pronunciation in the process, but he takes your utterance to mean that you are in agreement: the film crew is a disgrace.

You don't think you have ever worn a pleated skirt and a tailored long-sleeved blouse and scarf before, but you decide at this moment that you will do so more often. Usually the way you dress is not so different from the way the film crew is dressed, but now you see that the world—as represented by this manager at the Regency Hotel in Casablanca—sees you and treats you differently when you dress like this and apply makeup to cover the ridges of your skin. You are apologized to for things that don't merit an apology.

"We are trying to ask them to dress more appropriately for a hotel such as ours," the manager says, "but in the meantime I apologize for the inconvenience. Please let me know if I can be of help to you."

You stare at his face, memorizing his features: caramel eyes, a straight nose. You know that you might need him.

"Yes, thank you very much," you say. As you shake his hand to thank him for his offer, one of the crew members who is indeed sloppily dressed approaches the manager.

The man speaks in French to the manager and says there's a problem. You can't make out much else except for the word *drapeau.* Your brain picks out a definition you didn't know you had: *flag.*

There seems to be an issue with the flag flying outside the Regency Hotel. You notice you're lingering, so you walk away and approach the concierge desk, where an older gentleman in a crisp suit stares out at the lobby as though he's standing at the helm of a boat, observing an unextraordinary view.

You ask the concierge for directions to the embassy and he unfolds a small map. He circles the hotel, and circles the embassy, and hands you the map. You're relieved that the embassy appears close because you have no cash for a taxi. You will have to walk.

You step out of the hotel. No filming is currently happening. Men and women, dressed shabbily, are moving monitors around and adjusting wires while smoking dense, heavily packed cigarettes.

You walk in the direction of the embassy. The area surrounding the Regency is not much of a neighborhood; it's a grid of wide streets where people sell goods, many of which appear to have been stolen. You search absentmindedly for signs of your computer, your camera, still in its box. But this street is for the selling of stolen items that no one wants. An elderly toothless woman sits on an upside-down crate and displays a used and cracked asthma inhaler. A young man sells mix cassette tapes, their labels handwritten, some with hearts.

You walk to an enormous square and find hundreds of people gathered around. You ask one of the many guards what's going on. *"Qu'est-ce qui se passe?"* you say. But he doesn't understand the question. You question your French. You know you said it correctly. So you ask again. Still, he looks at you as though you should know.

Red Moroccan flags are everywhere—flying from every flagpole in the square, jutting out from buildings, hanging from balconies. You stand behind the rows of men in black leather jackets—they are almost all men—and a few children, who wait with eight-by-ten photos. You catch sight of one of the photos: it looks like a younger version of the king. Of course. *Le prince.* The prince.

Everyone around you is waiting for the prince himself.

Now you see a row of dignitaries lined up and you realize they too are there for the prince. You decide to remain where you are for a minute to see if you get a glimpse of him, before you keep moving.

You begin to feel stares as you stand there, the only Westerner in sight who's waiting for the prince. And the only woman. Where are the women? From your neck you remove your deep orange scarf, a scarf that you packed because it seemed Moroccan to you, or at least the shade of a Moroccan spice. You take it and wrap it around your head, covering much of your face. You dressed for the embassy, for the Regency but not for the street.

The scarf around your head cuts down on some of the stares, but still you are female. You wish you had an umbrella with you—it looks as though it might rain, and besides, an umbrella would allow you to hide. You decide to keep walking. It's almost 4 P.M. and you assume the embassy closes at 5. You don't have time to wait for the prince. You consult your map: the fastest route would be to walk across the square in front of you, but it's now blocked off for the prince's arrival, so you make your way around the large city block.

The neighborhood is in disrepair—benches are missing their seats, or tipped to the ground, the sidewalks are uneven. Grass is spotty and rare and no flowers have been planted. The people lingering in the streets where you walk are homeless or appear drunk. They don't seem to be aware, or else it doesn't mean anything to them, that nearby hundreds of people are awaiting their prince.

When you're almost all the way around the block, it starts to rain—first lightly, and then thrashingly. You duck under the canopy of a storefront for cover. Two men in leather jackets sprint out of the rain and under the canopy as well. They light cigarettes. The prince has still not arrived. More people are gathering and the guards are beginning to prohibit pedestrians from crossing the street.

Barricades have been erected, indicating down which streets the prince and his cavalcade will drive. Throngs of people stand in front of the silver railings. When the rain stops, which it does as suddenly as it started, you try to continue on your way to the embassy, but there are roadblocks everywhere.

You cross one street and take a right, only to find a barricade that forces you to retreat and take a different route. You endure the stares of people taking note of your skin, your body. Even an elderly grandmother holding the hand of a young boy gives you a stare that says, *You should not be here*.

You squeeze between two barricades and a policeman whistles. You raise your hand apologetically and move on. You need to keep moving.

Finally you make it to the embassy. It's 4:40. You're still wet from the rain. You should have brought an umbrella. A psychiatrist friend of yours once told you that a telltale sign of a mentally unstable person is she's never dressed appropriately for the weather. You decide to wait outside under the awning for another couple minutes to allow yourself to dry off even a little.

When you enter the embassy, you've never felt so happy to

see the American flag. You pass through the metal detector, and you're given a number. You sit in a folding chair waiting, surrounded by families and couples. You are the only one there by yourself. The room is small but regal, with flags and portraits. You stare at the photograph of Obama on the wall. He seems to care about you. Or is his look one of mild disappointment?

When your number is called, you approach window number three. An American woman in her forties, with a Sontag-gray streak in her dark hair, greets you. "How can I help you?" she says.

You find her formidable, and probably attribute more intelligence to her because of her Sontag streak, her streak of Susan Sontag.

"I'm an American citizen," you say. "I live in Florida. Usually. My passport and computer and everything were stolen by someone wearing a badge when I was checking into my hotel. The Golden Tulip."

"They were wearing a badge?" she says.

"Yes, but that was just a front."

"Have you been to the police?"

"Yes," you say. "They gave me another backpack that wasn't mine to replace my backpack. I mean, they thought they were giving me the right backpack. Or maybe they didn't think that. Anyway, I got the wrong backpack back. So now I have someone else's backpack and passport."

"Why would the police give you someone else's backpack?"

"I don't know," you say. "Maybe they were in on it."

"In on it with whom?"

"With the hotel."

"You're saying the Casablanca police and the Golden Tulip were in cahoots to steal your backpack."

It sounds ludicrous coming from her mouth.

"Yes," you say, suddenly less certain of anything, of everything.

"Can I see your ID?" she says.

"That's the thing: I don't have any ID. I just have this other backpack and passport, which I left at the hotel for safe-keeping."

"But why would you have someone else's backpack and passport?"

"Because the police gave it to me."

"Can I see the police report?" she says. "With your name on it."

"I don't have a police report."

"You don't have a police report," she says in disbelief.

"I have a document from them," you say. "With a red stamp from the police chief."

"Can I see it?" she asks.

You reach into your skirt pocket and extract the paper and unfold it.

It's blank.

You turn it over.

The other side is blank.

You feel your ears pop and widen, as though your sense of hearing will help you locate the document.

"I think I left it. I left the document at the hotel," you say, speaking slowly, trying to calm yourself down.

"And it has your name on it?"

"Yes," you lie, because you cannot believe you're in a situation where you have nothing with your own name on it.

"Can you get that document and bring it back here?" She is speaking to you like a child. Susan Sontag is speaking to you like a child.

"Yes," you say. "I'll get the police document and I'll bring it here."

"Bring it tomorrow," she says. "In the meantime, do you want to tell me whose passport and backpack they gave you? They were American, I assume?"

"Yes, she's American," you say.

"Her name?" she says.

You panic. If you give up Sabine Alyse's name you will have nothing.

You decide to lie because you have no choice: "I don't remember. I'll have to go back to the hotel and get that too," you say.

She looks at you skeptically, taking in your features for the first time. You imagine her describing you to someone else, perhaps the police, the ambassador, the secretary of state, the president. He will be so disappointed.

"You said you're staying at the Golden Tulip?" she says.

"Yes," you lie. "The Golden Tulip. I'll be there until this all gets resolved."

She scribbles something on a paper in front of her, a paper you cannot see. You imagine it's a list of suspicious persons, people she and the president are disappointed in.

"What time will you be back here tomorrow? What time can we expect to see you?"

"First thing," you say. You know you need to be agreeable. She suspects you of something and you need to be agreeable.

"Nine A.M.," she says.

"Perfect," you say.

"I'll take down your name so we're sure to have the appointment booked. What was your name again?"

She says this so casually that you know she suspects you, that she's trying to trap you. You give the name of a woman who helped you at the baggage store in Florida. You noted her name on the receipt. "Megan Willis," you say. It's the only name that comes to mind. Megan Willis is the one who suggested you purchase the basic black backpack, and that, when you really think about it, was the first true mistake. This all started with Megan Willis.

You walk casually out of the embassy door, and once you've exited you move quickly. Fuck, you think. This latest lie will be yet another thing you will have to explain when you return. You have no money to take a cab or bus, so once again you must walk. You wind through streets and pass through a small square where several policemen wearing dark black vests surround two groups of people. In the center of one circle is a woman; in the center of the other a man. The woman is crying and she's pointing at the man, and though you can't understand what she's saying, you know some sort of violation occurred. She gesticulates, using her hands to show the way the man fondled her rear. Two policemen are listening to the woman and another is holding the man by his arm.

You watch and then, as though reminded that you too are a woman, you move on.

As you continue to walk to your hotel, you think of how fortuitous it was that Sabine Alyse didn't cancel her credit cards. And then you wonder why a woman who has a AAA card in her wallet and shops at J.Crew and strikes you as a fairly together woman wouldn't cancel her credit cards when she discovered her backpack with her wallet and passport were missing. You got the backpack this morning, so she's been missing it for at least that long. You canceled your cards within an hour. You contemplate what might have prevented her from making the calls you made to Vipul and Christy. Maybe Sabine is somewhere where she can't make calls. She's been kidnapped. You picture her blindfolded. She could be dead. And what if the embassy knows she's dead? What if the embassy finds you, and her backpack on you? Wouldn't they assume you did it? Wouldn't they assume at the very least that you stole her possessions?

No. No. This is madness. She's not dead. And you have a document proving the police gave you her possessions. The document is everything. And it's back in the hotel.

As you approach the Regency you see a line of people formed as though they're protesters, but they're not shouting anything; they're just staring. It's the prince, you think. He must be at the Regency.

But as you get closer and make your way through the line, you see filming is now taking place at the entrance to the hotel. You explain to a guard that you're a guest at the Regency, and he informs you that you'll have to wait a few minutes before you can enter. He apologizes.

You move closer to the entrance of the hotel and join other guests who are watching the filming. You are vibrating, almost jogging in place. You need to find that piece of paper with the red stamp. But instead you are forced to watch the filming of a movie.

The scene being shot involves a woman on an old bicycle as she rides up to the front entrance of the hotel and disembarks. Then she does it again. And a third time. Lights are adjusted. Cameras are pulled forward and back on a trolley.

You find yourself enjoying this. Its repetitions are soothing. And now you are sure the document is on the desk, in your room, where you left it. It's in the Regency, and all is safe within the Regency. The director says, "Cut!"

After the woman disembarks for the fourth time, she takes off what you realize is a long, dark black wig with bangs. Beneath the wig her hair is brown, like yours, and pulled back into a tight bun. You recognize her. She's the young woman you saw emerging from the hotel elevator when you first checked in. You had no idea she was a movie star. She doesn't look like a movie star. She looks like you: same height, same plain face. She disappears into the hotel and the bike is rolled out of view, back where it came from. Seconds later, another young woman is on the bike.

The cameras start rolling but now it is this other woman with black hair who is on the bike, cycling up to the front of the hotel. She disembarks. You see that this woman resembles a famous American actress. And then it hits you: this is a famous American actress. Her face has been on the covers of so many magazines, and yet, even at this distance you can tell she's more beautiful, more delicate, more bizarrely perfect in real life.

She retreats and a crew member walks the bicycle out of sight. A minute later she rides up again. Everyone on set is more focused, more engaged now that it's the famous American actress on the bicycle.

She does three takes and on the fourth take her foot falls off the pedal and the pedal spins and she laughs. A makeup woman wearing a short, brush-filled apron, rushes out and uses a wet wipe on the famous American actress's leg, removing any grease. Another woman who is so elaborately dressed you guess she must be from the costume department emerges from the side of the set and adjusts the right fold at the bottom of the movie star's pedal pushers. A crew member walks the bike back to the starting point. Then the movie star rides up to the front of the hotel again and this time doesn't send the pedal spinning. When the scene is finished, she raises her hands in the victory sign—she can ride a bike without messing up a scene! The crew around her claps, and she gives an exaggerated and theatrical bow.

You have read a few magazine profiles about this famous American actress and now you think that they haven't done her justice. In real life she is more beautiful, yes, but also very human, very funny. She is capable of making fun of herself, of her mistakes on set, and the crew applauds this. You haven't been on any movie sets before, but you are fairly positive that everyone on this set is in awe of the famous American actress, and everyone likes her more than they expected to. There's an earnestness in the way they surround her afterward. The director approaches and puts his arm around her in a fatherly way.

Filming appears to be done for now, at this location at least. The famous American actress is ushered into the Regency, but a transformation has occurred: she's no longer a girl biking up to the entrance of a hotel; she's an American movie star once more, and now she's surrounded by two men who, if you're not mistaken, must be her bodyguards. They whisk her past the onlookers in the lobby and into an elevator that is miraculously waiting. Is there a third bodyguard inside who timed it so that the doors would open just when she appeared? The swiftness with which she enters the lobby and is lifted up to what is surely the best room is so well orchestrated it makes everything that happened on the film set look like it was done by amateurs—shabbily dressed amateurs.

You take the next elevator to your room. You can picture the document on the desk. You made copies and brought them back to your room, right? You cannot remember the order of the settings of the day's events: embassy, business center, police station, Golden Tulip, Regency. They're just images on a scattered deck of cards.

A bottle of champagne sits in a bucket of ice on your desk. You read the card, which is addressed to Sabine. "Wishing you a pleasant stay," the card says. "Warmly, your grateful manager."

You search the desk for the document. It's not on the desk. It's not near the desk, under the desk. You throw the comforter from the bed. You open and close the curtains. You look behind the television, in the closets, in your suitcase. It's not in the room.

You sit in the desk chair defeated. You eye the champagne. You want a glass to calm your nerves. You struggle with the cork. There's something wrong. You turn the cork toward you and study it. You pull at it and it hits you in the chest and the champagne follows, dampening your blouse and skirt.

"Jesus!" you say aloud. You hold your hand to your chest. You feel like you've been shot. Your hands are sticky and your clothes are wet. You can smell the dried rose scent of the champagne on your scarf, and you untangle it from your neck. Your blouse clings to your skin as you take it off, and you unzip your skirt and let it drop to the floor. You rummage through your suitcase for whatever is available and easy. You pull on a dull, wrinkled T-shirt, some black spandex exercise pants.

You try to think. A phone rings in the room next to yours. You remember the man and his annoying cell phone ring at the business center. That's where you left the original. It must still be there. You slide on your sneakers and pick up your key card.

The elevator ride is interminable. It seems to stop at every floor to let in another hotel guest. The guests are inevitably well dressed, and carry suitcases or purses of fine leather. The purses are bright-colored citron or red; gold Chanel or Hermès logos dangle from their zippers.

You should never have bought a simple black backpack.

You should have picked a fluorescent knockoff Hermès bag with metallic charms hanging from its multiple zippers. Then the thief would never have been able to walk out of the hotel so casually, the black unisex backpack flung over his shoulder.

You exit the elevator and go straight to the business center. You lift up the top of the copier. No paper is inside. You check the mouth of the machine for the copy.

Nothing. You never pressed copy. Or did you? You made one copy but it was blank. You turned over the police report. The man with the phone distracted you. And you left. Now the police report is gone.

You flee the business center; the door slams behind you.

You approach reception, and the long-haired woman standing behind the desk says, "Are you looking for the fitness center?"

"No," you say, confused, until you understand that the only possible explanation for your attire is that you're going to work out.

"Actually," you say, because saying that word calms you down, makes you not—you hope—come across as frantic as you feel. "By mistake I left a very important document in the copy machine earlier today, and now it's not there."

"You are sure you left it there?"

"Yes," you say. "Has anyone turned anything in?"

"I don't think so," the long-haired woman says. She rummages below the reception desk. "Nothing here."

She calls over to a short-haired woman working one com-

puter down from her. The short-haired woman looks at the
desk area around her and shrugs.

"No," says the long-haired woman. "Nothing's been
turned in."

"Is there a lost and found?" you ask.

"A what?"

"A place that people put things that are lost? So other
guests can find them?"

"This is that place," says the woman.

"What about housekeeping?" you say. "Do they clean the
business center?"

"Yes, but they shouldn't take anything." Before you have
to ask her to do so, she calls housekeeping. You feel she's on
your side.

She speaks in Arabic and waits. She moves the phone away
from her mouth. "They're checking," she tells you.

You wait for two minutes while they check.

She speaks into the phone and hangs up.

"No, nothing," she says.

You go back into the business center and look at each computer station. You peer under the lid of the photocopier: nothing.

You pass by the woman working at the currency-exchange
booth. You have an idea.

You approach the glass window. "Have you seen anyone
come out of the business center carrying papers this afternoon?"

"*Pardonnez-moi?*" she says, leaning in closer to the glass.

You repeat yourself, speaking louder.

"You are asking me if anyone left the business center carrying papers?"

"Yes," you say.

"Everyone leaves the business center carrying papers. That is where they print their papers."

You have never liked the currency-exchange woman and now you actively loathe her.

You decide to find the manager. He knows you and will understand your predicament.

You walk to the front of the hotel, where he is in conversation with the sloppily dressed crew member again. He does not look pleased. The crew member looks more shabbily dressed now than he did earlier.

You stand near them, lingering. The manager must feel your gaze because he looks up.

"The fitness center is that way," he says, and points.

"Thank you," you say. "I actually need help with something else."

"One moment, please," he says, and continues a heated negotiation with the crew member.

"You cannot film in the lobby on Monday," the manager says. "We have a very important conference checking in on Monday and your film crew cannot be the first thing they see when they enter the Regency."

The crew member starts to protest.

"You can do it Tuesday, but not Monday," the manager says. "We will have explained the situation and the relaxed dress code to our guests by then."

The conversation ends and it's your turn.

"Thank you for the champagne," you say.

He stares at you, evidently not recognizing you in your spandex.

"You had champagne sent to my room."

"Oh, yes," he says. He seems to be questioning why he bothered.

"I have a bit of a situation," you say. "My belongings were stolen at the Golden Tulip yesterday. I was originally supposed to stay there."

"You were going to stay there instead of here?" He questions your judgment, your taste, your budget. Your wrinkled and faded gym attire isn't helping.

"Yes, and my backpack was stolen and I went to the police station and they gave me a report with a red stamp. A very important red stamp. I went to make copies in the business center and I must have left it behind because I don't have it now. I'm so tired. I just arrived yesterday and so much has happened . . ."

"You are looking for a piece of paper?" he says.

"Yes."

"What is your name again?"

You give him Sabine's name.

"If we find a piece of paper with your name on it, we will call you immediately," he tells you.

Back in your room you check the champagne bottle to see if there's anything left. A quarter of the bottle. You fill your glass and finish it quickly.

Your thoughts become slower, more orderly. You lied to the embassy woman. You told her you were Megan Willis.

You told her you had a document from the police, but now you don't. It seems impossible to go back to the embassy without your own identification, with only the possessions of Sabine Alyse. And having given Susan Sontag a fabricated name. But without the embassy what can you do? You cannot return to the police station: when the police chief pressed his warted thumb into your thumb you knew he was saying that you were to never see each other again. You doubt he will defend you if you return to the station. You will have to continue to be Sabine Alyse, here at the Regency. You will have to eat here, charge everything to the room. But how long will that last? How long before Sabine Alyse's credit-card charges are traced to you?

You stand in front of the window, looking out at Casablanca as it presents itself below. A modern tram snakes through the city. You pour yourself the last of the champagne and stare out at the clock in the distance: it's 10 P.M. You stop noticing anything new. You simply focus on the patterns pedestrians make as they crisscross through the square below. Unlike your sister, whose brain is a beehive, and who has excelled at continuously plotting her next step, you have always been good at staring out of windows for long periods of time. You try not to calculate how much of your life you have wasted doing exactly what you are doing now.

In the morning you shower and wash your hair, using the small hotel bottles. Yesterday they made you smell like someone else but today they smell like you. At home you wear something floral. This new scent you've adopted smells of tangerines and honey. The robe is back on a hanger, its sash tied at the waist once more. As you untie the belt you feel as though you're undressing someone else.

You are too hungry to wait for room service. In the lobby you approach a waiter and ask where you sit if you want food. He says anywhere. He tells you one side of the lobby is non-smoking, the other smoking. There's no wall between the two.

You order coffee and an omelet, and look around you, catching shards of conversation. Businessmen chatter over cappuccinos in French, Portuguese, and Arabic. Five women dressed in high heels and showing bare calves have arranged themselves around another table. If you didn't know better you would think they'd come to Casablanca to celebrate one of their fortieth birthdays. But you know better. No one comes to Casablanca to celebrate anything. Your guidebook to Mo-rocco (also in your backpack) was right: the first thing you should do upon arrival in Casablanca is get out of Casablanca.

Which is what you're trying to do. But you're not sure where you'll go. Your plan was to go to Fez, to Marrakech, to the desert, but these places no longer have appeal. You try to imagine when they did have appeal. You try to remember the person you were when planning this very trip.

Across the lobby, in the nonsmoking section, you see the woman who slightly resembles you. The stand-in for the fa-mous American actress. She's not wearing the wig. She's sitting with two other people you haven't seen before. The woman is older; she is pale, professional, precise. She wears practical but expensive shoes that have low square heels, and her hair is cut short in the style favored by women who don't want to make a fuss, who don't want to present themselves as overly feminine. She is perhaps fifty. The man sitting with her is an unlikely match: he's wearing black jeans and a white shirt and has tattoos on his arms. The stand-in appears to be crying.

The tattooed man and the pale practical woman seem agitated with the stand-in. They are reprimanding her, and you assume that their words are the cause of her tears. What has she done? Who are these people causing her to sob? Still, as she buries her head in her hands it's clear why she's a stand-in and not an actress; her gestures are dramatic, obvious choices.

You are two tables away and wish you were closer. You wonder what is happening. Witnessing someone else's troubles right now is a very welcome distraction.

The waiter approaches with your omelet and coffee. You stare at the basket of bread and scoot yourself forward on the chair. The waiter steps away for a moment and returns with an oversize suede pillow from a nearby couch and places it behind you so that you can comfortably reach the table, so you don't have to sit on the edge of the seat.

"*Merci,*" you say.

With the first sip of coffee your mind begins to work through your options. Is going to the embassy out of the question? Yes, you have no police document. You could be under suspicion the moment you walk in. Susan Sontag made note of you. She could have obtained your photo from the security cameras.

By now, Sabine Alyse's credit cards have probably either

been reported, or if she's suffered a fate as terrible as you fear she might have, you are certain that there will be inquiries about what happened to her. You should not be staying at a hotel under her name. You cannot stay another night at this hotel.

As you finish your coffee, the waiter comes and refills your cup. You start thinking that it's madness to be in this lobby at all. Every minute that you're sitting here increases the likelihood that if anyone's looking for clues as to what happened to Sabine Alyse, and to her backpack, they will find you here. At the very least, you will be charged with stealing her possessions. At worst, you will be charged with playing a part in whatever happened to her.

The tattooed man seems to be repeatedly glancing over at you. Why is he staring at you? He looks as though he could be a security guard. The stand-in gets up and leaves. The tattooed man talks intensely to the pale professional woman, and now she's looking at you too. She looks like she could be in the CIA. No one else in the lobby wears shoes like hers, no one else wears their hair in the style she does.

Something's wrong. They know something about you and Sabine Alyse.

You tell yourself you're being overly suspicious of them. You tell yourself to look down at your food for ten seconds. You tell yourself that if they're still staring at you when you look up then they are onto you. If they've looked away, you can relax.

You stare at your plate. You count the seconds. When you look up they are staring at you more intently than before, while having a very serious discussion.

You have to leave the restaurant. You have to leave without paying. You can't sign Sabine's name again. You need to go to your room and pack your things and get out of this hotel.

You try not to run as you make your way across the lobby and up the elevator to your room. You place the backpack—the evidence—inside your suitcase, and throw your clothes and toiletries on top. You zip up the suitcase and make your way to the elevator.

But you can't go downstairs. The pale professional woman and the tattooed man are there. The manager is there. By now they might have all figured out who you are—or aren't.

Inside the elevator you see the button for the rooftop pool. You'll go there, wait an hour or two until the people who were so interested in you have left the lobby.

The elevator opens directly to the pool. You walk out with your suitcase. The pool is a blue square without a diving board. You sit on a chaise longue. The sun is not yet warm enough for sunbathers and there's only one swimmer in the pool, a woman. She stops swimming and looks at you. You can see she's wondering what you're doing there, fully dressed with a suitcase.

You think quickly and find the door to the women's locker room. You wait in there. Then you realize how strange this is. The woman in the pool could report that there's a woman who entered the changing room and never left.

Your only option to appear as normal as possible is to swim. And besides: swimming has always soothed you. You remove a dark blue one-piece from your suitcase. You didn't bother packing a bikini because you feared it would only mock your body in its current condition. You pull on the blue swimsuit and hoist the front up over your chest, and adjust the elastic down over your rear. You stash your suitcase under a massage table that for some reason is in the changing room. Maybe they bring it outside on nice days for poolside massages.

You dive from the edge of the pool where it says NO DIVING, and swim underwater to the other side, not once coming up for air. The water is a good temperature, neither too cold nor too warm. You are not a casual swimmer. You competed on swim teams starting when you were eight, and you attended college on a diving scholarship. You swim quick laps and realize that you are following the other woman, that you're too close to her feet. You slow down your strokes so it doesn't appear that you're chasing her.

The woman gets out of the pool. She goes into the changing room and a minute later leaves the pool area via the elevator.

You swim twenty more laps without stopping. You relish your turns, the way you glide as you push off from the edges of the pool. You've always gained speed on turns; they've long been your secret asset as a swimmer. You can feel your mind being cleared. Water does this to you.

You towel off your shins and arms thoroughly, the way you did with a shammy before your next competitive dive. When you look up you see two other hotel guests exiting the elevator. As they approach, both fully dressed in pants and shirts, your heart seizes. It's the couple from the lobby, the pale practical woman and the tattooed man.

You glance around to see if they could possibly have another objective than to talk. Nothing and no one is around you.

"Hello!" the practical woman calls out. You see her face change to a smile. You realize she's performing for you.

"Hello!" the tattooed man shouts.

You wave hello. A smooth motion of your hand, as though you're wiping the front window of a car.

You pull the towel around your chest, tucking one edge into the top of the other so the bulk of your body is concealed. It seems strange to be wearing a swimsuit while they are clothed. And why are they approaching you? You consider fleeing to the locker room. Was there an exit there? You can't recall.

The unlikely duo sits down on the chaise longue next to yours. "Sorry to interrupt your swim," says the pale practical woman, not seeming at all sorry.

"Yes, our apologies," says the tattooed man, seeming a little more apologetic. His tattoos bear words in Arabic and one, DESTINY, in English. He speaks with a slight British accent. Your guess is he studied in London as an exchange student. Now it all makes sense. They work for Interpol. You eye the elevator door, assessing whether if you run, you can escape. But the tattooed man looks athletic. You have no chance.

"We saw you downstairs," the pale practical woman says. "Did you see us?"

What is the right answer? The pale practical woman is American. Maybe she works for the embassy. She's one of Sontag's minions.

"No," you lie. "Maybe."

The tattooed man says, "We were in the lobby. We noticed you across the room. Are you staying here in the hotel?"

This is a trap. You need a lawyer. You shouldn't answer any of these questions.

"Yes," you say. You need to end this conversation. "Excuse me, I'm in the middle of my laps . . . I was going to go back in."

"I'm sorry," the pale practical woman says. "We're being so cryptic."

"We're making a movie," the tattooed man says. "You might have seen our crew?"

Could this be true? Could these two be members of the film crew instead of intelligence operatives? You begin to relax.

"I think so," you say.

"It's a medium-budget film with a major American movie star," the pale practical woman says.

"What's your name?" the pale practical woman says.

What *is* your name? Sabine Alyse? Megan Willis?

"Reeves Conway," you say. It's the name of your sister's baby. She is two months old. You feel closer to her than anyone else in the world.

"Nice to meet you, Reeves," the tattooed man says, without introducing himself. "What brings you to Morocco?"

"Vacation," you say.

"How nice," the pale practical woman says. You can tell she doesn't think much of vacations; they're probably a waste of time for her. "Are you here alone?"

"Yes."

"And you're from the States? Canada?" the pale practical woman asks.

You still have no idea what they want from you.

"Florida," you say, telling the truth.

"How long will you be out here?" the pale practical woman asks.

"I'm not sure," you say. You were supposed to go back in ten days, but now you really don't know how that will happen.

They look at each other and the pale practical woman nods. A decision seems to have been made.

"We have a proposal for you," the tattooed man says.

"A proposal?" you say. It sounds illegal as you repeat his words back to him.

"A job offer," says the pale practical woman. "Please hear us out."

"Okay," you say, tentatively. You have no money and no ability to access money. You had not thought of getting a job, but now it seems logical, necessary.

The woman clears her throat, as if about to say something very discreet, very important. "I am the personal secretary to the actress starring in the film," she says.

She waits for you to say something, for you to be impressed.

"Okay," you say.

She studies you as you say this, and the calmness of your response seems to please her.

The tattooed man jumps in. "I'm not sure if you know much about how it works with a film, but with the big stars we have stand-ins. The stand-ins help us block the scene so that we can make sure the lighting and the camera angles are correct before we bring the star out. This helps with several factors. Firstly, we make sure the star does not exhaust himself or herself . . . in this case clearly we're making sure that she does not exhaust herself. Secondly, we limit the number of onlookers who have time to spread the gossip that the star is appearing. If the star comes out first, then it gives every person standing on the street the chance to text and tweet and before long"—he snaps loudly here—"we have a mob situation."

The pale practical woman is looking at him disapprovingly, impatiently. This appears to be the natural state of her face. When he glances over at her she smiles at him.

You are wondering what any of this has to do with you.

"You are probably wondering what this has to do with you," the pale practical woman says.

You shrug, as though you have been enjoying a story and have no concern or intrigue as to why you are being told this story.

"The young woman, Ivy, who has been playing the stand-in has had an emergency and has to fly home," the tattooed man says.

"It's unlikely she'll be returning," says the practical woman.

"We are a Moroccan crew and don't have anyone who resembles the movie star in skin color, height, or size, but we think you might be right," says the tattooed man.

"Should we continue talking?" the pale practical woman asks.

"Yes," you say.

They both look relieved.

"Great," the tattooed man says. "I can imagine how bizarre this must all sound to you. We were just getting desperate and we saw you alone and—"

The practical woman cuts him off. She has no time for stories of desperation, especially now that she senses a possible solution.

"Can I ask how tall you are?" asks the practical woman.

"Five foot seven," you answer.

The tattooed man looks at the practical woman. She tells him that the actress is five foot six and a half. "So that's . . ." The Moroccan man uses his thumb and forefinger to try to measure how big a gap half an inch is.

"Less than that," says the practical woman.

He, who is not used to measuring outside of the metric system, brings his thumb and forefinger together.

"That's okay," he says to the practical woman.

"Yes, I think so," she says.

She turns to you. Suddenly you are involved in their conversation again. "You will have to wear flats on set."

"And a wig," says the tattooed man to the pale practical secretary. To you he says: "Your hair is a little short, not dark enough. Also the movie takes place in the sixties. It's a period film. The wig will help."

"Yes," the pale practical secretary says, "she should just use Ivy's wig. I'll make a note of the wig for the costume department." She takes out her iPhone and makes a note of it.

"You probably have some questions about the job," says the practical woman.

You have no questions. You want this job.

"Yes," you say. "I have a couple."

They stare at you, expectantly.

"When would the position start?"

"You'd probably meet her this afternoon. Just to get to know each other," the pale practical secretary says. "Unfortunately I don't know if you'll meet the director today. He's attending to some personal business."

The tattooed man glances at her, and smiles. She does not smile back. You wonder about the nature of the personal business he's attending to.

"You'll meet the security guards," the practical secretary says. "They'd have to get to know you."

"You may have seen them with her around the hotel," the tattooed man says.

You nod. You want to ask about pay, when and how much, and are about to ask, when the practical secretary preempts you.

"You'd be paid in cash. Long story," she says.

Your mouth drops open. You close it.

"You'll be paid five hundred dollars a day, at the end of each week," the practical woman says. "This week will be prorated given we're almost halfway through it."

She must have misread the expression on your face as one of alarm, of concern, because the practical woman says, "And of course we'd cover your accommodations." Then she frowns. "Unfortunately we don't have it in the budget for you to continue staying at the Regency."

"Where would I go?" you say. You cannot return to the Golden Tulip.

"There's a hotel next door called the Grand," says the tattooed man. "It's not so grand but it's where the crew stays. We have a whole block of rooms."

Your mind is strangely sharp—you attribute this to your

swim—and you find yourself working two steps ahead. You know you cannot check into this new hotel under Sabine's name. You cannot check in under Reeves's name. You have no way to check in under any name—not without a passport. You can't even meet anyone at the front desk. But the stand-in who is leaving surely has a room, and has surely vacated it.

"This is a lot to take in," you say. "So I'd have to pack all my things up, leave this hotel, go through the whole check-in hassle?" You widen your eyes, as if all this would surely overwhelm you—you must make them believe you are a woman of leisure for whom all of this moving and working will be an unfamiliar hardship.

The practical secretary takes the bait. "We'd have someone come grab your bags. And they'd just bring them to Ivy's old room. Which would be cleaned up of course. No check-in, nothing. The hotel's been very good to us. They leave us all alone."

No check-in, you think. This is a relief on a dozen levels.

"You're probably wondering how many days your services will be required before you can go back home, or wherever your next destination is," says the practical woman.

It has not occurred to you to wonder about this. "Yes, of course," you say.

"Filming is scheduled for three more weeks," the tattooed man says.

"Some nights go very late, but you will get two days off a week," the practical woman adds.

"Three weeks," you repeat absentmindedly.

They stare at you. You are their last hope. You know you

should up the price, but you have nothing; you're not in a position to barter.

"That works for my schedule," you say, as though you have a schedule.

"Great," says the tattooed man. He is elated.

"Now, let's make sure you two meet and that she feels she can work with you," says the pale practical secretary. She glances at her phone; she scrolls. "Oh, wow. Something just changed. She could meet you in twenty minutes in the tenth-floor lounge."

"The tenth-floor lounge?" you say.

"It's on the tenth floor," she says. "It's private," she adds, and rises. She's short in her practical heels.

You stand, still wrapped in your towel. You wipe your moist palm on the towel before shaking hands with each of them.

You go into the dressing room, and lie down on the massage table, facing the ceiling. You are happy for the time to think.

You needed to stop using Sabine Alyse's name and credit card. This job allows you to do that.

You needed to get out of this hotel, which was going to be difficult without identification. This job satisfies that.

And you will be paid.

You roll off the massage table. To secure the job you should try to make yourself resemble the famous actress in whatever way possible. You noticed the previous stand-in, the one you will be replacing, the one you saw crying—why was she crying?—dressed in jeans and a blouse and heels. You realize she must have been shorter than the famous actress, so she needed heels to replicate the famous actress's height; you need anything without a heel.

You select metallic sandals from your suitcase (you packed them in case you ended up in the desert, or on a beach), jeans you didn't think you'd be wearing in Morocco, and a black cotton blouse. You've noticed the famous American actress often wears black. She was in edgy independent movies when she started her film career, and she seems to want to remind the public of that fact.

You dress and then stand in front of the mirror to apply the makeup you bought at the Casablanca beauty store. Your skin. If only the marks were small pits that together could form a star. That might be interesting, even. You would settle for that. Instead: there's a reason that for most of your life you've run and swam. There's a reason why you finally arrived at diving as your competitive sport. With diving your face was virtually unseen. It was all about the shape your body made in the distance as you dropped from a high board and disappeared deep into the water. By the time you came up for air, the judges had determined their score. It had nothing to do with your face.

When you are finished dressing you look in the mirror. First to make sure your clothes look right, then a second time to make sure you appear sane. The third time to see how much you resemble her. You pull your hair back in a ponytail, so there's less of it, and because you saw Ivy wearing her hair in that style. She wore her hair pulled back so the wig could easily go on and off.

You practice saying your niece's name twice in front of the

mirror. "Reeves Conway. Reeves Conway." Then you use it in a sentence. "Hello, I'm Reeves Conway."

It suits you. More than your own name does.

You stash your suitcase under the massage table because you don't know where else to put it. You take a towel from a stack and drape it over the suitcase.

You exit the dressing room and wait for the elevator. When it arrives, you step inside and press ten.

The elevator doors open and the lounge is in front of you. With low couches and an enormous TV and international newspapers set out, it's a miniature version of the lounge on the first floor. But the only person in the lounge is a bartender. He stands before a bar lined with large backlit bottles and oranges in vases.

The bartender greets you in English and in French. You ask for a glass of sparkling water, and sit down on one of the plush sofas and wait. You worry you look too desperate, sitting there facing the elevator doors, as though waiting to pounce the moment they open and the famous actress emerges. You move to another couch.

The bartender brings you a tall narrow glass of sparkling water and it tastes so refreshing you already know you want another one. This is how it is in these countries—the glasses are so small and you are always thirsty. At the home you shared with your husband your cups were bowls, but your thirst was never satisfied.

The elevator doors haven't opened but now the famous American actress is in the lounge. She must be staying on this floor, you realize. Suddenly she is before you. She is radiant, as though she has swallowed a light, a sun, and is glowing from within. She's small-boned, tiny. Her eyes are the green of damp moss; her hair darker than it's been in other films. The fringe of bangs is new—you assume it's been styled this way for this shoot. Her cheeks are wide and her nose narrow. You have to work to not stare.

"Hi," she says.

Just like that. Hi.

You stand up, and as you do so, you hit your knee on the glass coffee table. You act as though you didn't.

You shake her hand and you say your name is Reeves and she says her name, which, momentarily, strikes you as funny. There are few people in the world who don't know her name.

Her bodyguards are close—one is already standing by the bartender, the other by the elevator. They are so stealthy they appear suddenly, like magicians in a trick. One is Latino and the other pale with red hair. They don't look at you head-on, but out of the corners of their eyes, they are watching you. The famous American actress doesn't acknowledge they're there. You assume they have been with her for years.

She flops down on the couch, elegantly. You have seen her image a million times and still this is new. You understand, instantaneously, what it is to have presence. You can't keep your eyes off her features—so much smaller than you would have expected—and her skin, so much smoother than any skin you've seen. She doesn't have a single indentation on her face, except for a dimple below her left cheek when she smiles her endearingly lopsided smile. Her dimple is famous. You wonder if she's had it insured.

"Where are you from?" she asks.

"Florida originally, but then I went to New York, and now I'm in Florida."

"I love New York," she says.

"What about you?" you ask, though you know she lives in L.A.

"L.A.," she says.

You nod as though this is new information you're taking in.

"I'm so fucking exhausted," she says.

"Late night of work?" Now you're talking. The two of you are just talking.

"Yeah, we went until one A.M. And then I come home and this fucking possessive boyfriend of mine wants to argue."

You know who the boyfriend is, of course. You wonder if she should be telling you this.

"I'm sorry," you say. "That's the worst."

"It is, right? Are you involved with anyone right now?" she asks.

"Um, no," you say, taken off guard. "I'm the opposite."

"Bad breakup?" she asks. She pulls her legs up onto the couch and leans into you. She looks like an actress in a movie who's acting interested. You can't separate how genuine her interest is, or how much she's playing the part of someone who's interested. It occurs to you that maybe she can't tell the difference either. Maybe for her the line is very thin.

"My husband and I are splitting up," you tell her. "I decided to leave him."

"How long ago?" she asks.

"Two months ago . . . or so. I've lost track." You know it's been exactly nine weeks.

"Are you definitely divorcing?"

"Yes," you say. "I've filed the papers. There's no way we'll ever . . ."—you search for the polite word—"reconcile."

"Wow," she says. "That's so impressive that you're leaving him."

"I hadn't exactly thought of it that way," you say. " 'Excruciating' is the word that comes to mind." Even that word does not come close to describing the intensity of pain you feel.

She crosses her legs in the other direction. She leans in again to ask her next question: "Did you have kids together?"

"Together" is a haunting word. You did little together.

"No," you say, knowing she'll say that's a relief.

"Well, that's a relief."

You nod, and think for a moment of your sister's baby. Reeves.

"You're getting divorced, you're surviving. It's part of your story now," the famous American actress says.

"I guess so," you say. You don't volunteer that on most days you don't feel like you're surviving. "I wish I didn't feel so fucking angry at him. What he did makes me feel like I failed at something enormous. In the minds of people who knew us—and even people who didn't—I failed. It's horrific and humiliating on so many levels."

"Humiliating? No. If I were getting divorced, I'd go around saying, 'Hey, guess what, I'm only in my twenties but I'm getting divorced! And I'm alive. Take that, motherfuckers.' "

You are reminded that you have read about her filthy mouth.

"Take that, motherfuckers," you mutter, under your breath.

She laughs. It's a genuine laugh. And a terrible one. It's a cackle. You don't think you've ever heard it in her films. You would have noticed.

"Think of it this way, Reeves," she says. "Everyone's scared of getting divorced but you're doing it. You're getting it out of the way and now you can move on with your life."

"I can move on with my life," you repeat.

"I might get married just so I can get divorced and get it over with," she says.

You laugh, instinctively, genuinely. The famous American actress is much more interesting than you thought she'd be.

"You have a point," you say.

"If I were you I'd get married again as fast as possible so that I could get divorced a second time."

She looks over your shoulder, and stares at something. You turn to follow her gaze. She's staring at the bartender, who's Moroccan, maybe twenty-five. He's polishing a glass that already looks polished and is placing it back on the shelf.

"He's pretty cute," she says.

"Not bad," you agree. "You think he'd marry me?"

"Totally," she says. "Can I throw a lingerie bridal shower for you? I fucking live for lingerie. And cotton grandma panties. Depends on the day."

The pale practical secretary enters the room, and sees you laughing and the famous American actress cackling. You wonder if the pale practical secretary has grown accustomed to the actress's terrible laugh. You wonder if it's ever possible to grow accustomed to it.

"Am I late?" she asks, looking at her watch. She answers her own question. "You two were both early." She looks distressed.

She sits down on a chair between the two couches where you and the famous American actress are seated.

"Would you like something to drink?" she asks the actress.

"A small coffee," she says, and the practical secretary waves the bartender over and orders two coffees.

"Are you feeling better than you were this morning?" the practical secretary asks. She is at least twenty years older than the famous American actress, and it's somewhat disconcerting to see her catering to someone so much younger than herself.

"Still exhausted." The actress looks at you and offers an explanation. "That fucking boyfriend."

The practical secretary shoots the actress an admonishing look.

"What?" the famous American actress says. "I already told her all about it."

The practical secretary's face tightens.

"I trust her," the famous American actress says.

"Thanks," you say, because it does seem like a compliment.

"You're welcome," says the actress, and laughs her strange laugh.

You smile because you're afraid if you don't your face will express your alarm at her terrible laugh. In return, she smiles her big, notorious smile and you feel like you're in one of her movies. Whenever she smiles like that on-screen, the person she is smiling at is instantly charmed.

The pale practical secretary clears her throat. "Did either of you want to talk to her?" the practical secretary asks, looking at the bodyguards.

You had almost forgotten about them. Now you understand how the famous American actress can act as though they don't exist.

The bodyguards lock eyes with each other and appear unsure, but then the one with the red hair says: "Yes."

The pale practical secretary and the famous actress move to one side of the couch and the secretary pulls out a schedule she wants to run by the actress.

For a moment you're alone. But then the bodyguard with the red hair comes over and sits across from you. He's not a large man; he wears a puffy brown leather jacket and you're sure he wears it to give him more heft. The other bodyguard keeps watch on the elevator doors, on the bartender, on you.

The red-haired bodyguard stares at your naked left hand and asks if you're married.

You tell him you're getting divorced.

He asks about the man who you're divorcing and you tell him that he's still in Florida, that you're the one who moved out.

"No pets?" he says, revealing he's heard the conversation about kids; why else would he jump to the topic of pets?

"I used to have a turtle," you tell him. "But I had to feed it a salad every day for lunch. It was a lot of food preparation."

He nods. "I'm studying turtles right now. Galápagos and Darwin and evolution."

"You're a Darwin fan," you say.

"Oh, I wouldn't go that far," he says, as though you really have pushed a boundary. "People assume Darwin was right about evolution being gradual, but I'm intrigued by radical speciation." He looks away but has you in the corners of his eyes.

"What's that?" you say, not because you're necessarily interested, but because you want to do well at this interview and you believe that this entails having a conversation that makes this man feel intriguing.

"It's also known as punctuated equilibrium," he says. "Does that sound familiar?"

It doesn't. "Maybe," you say. "Can you remind me?"

He sits up straighter on the couch, like he's being interviewed for a documentary. "There are these periods in evolution when species are in stasis because there's no need for change. But then, usually because of a change in their environment, they have to adapt rapidly. That's how new species come about."

"What kind of environmental change?" you ask. As a twin, you've always been interested in nature versus nurture. Also, if you keep him talking about this he won't ask about you.

"I'm glad you asked. I'll give you an example," he says, and then pauses, as though deciding which one to give. "Say there's a species of birds—there are these beautiful ones I'm interested in right now. They're tropical-looking in color, their wings have orange, white, and blue in them. Anyway, they existed for thousands of years, and took shelter in a particular kind of tree. I can't remember the name of the tree right now," he says, and his hand makes a fist.

"That's okay," you say. "Go on."

"So the tree where they build their nests and lay their eggs gets suddenly infected by this bacteria. And the trees start to die. So what do the birds do then?"

You realize he's posing this question to you.

"Find another tree?" you offer.

He points at you, as though he's been lecturing a class and you're the pupil who called out the right answer.

"But what if these new trees are taller and the birds need to be able to fly higher up to lay their eggs. Then what happens?" he says.

You open your mouth but realize that this time he doesn't want you to answer.

"They have to adapt," he continues. "They have to have greater wing strength. The birds that don't have it die off, and the others adapt and the species selects to have greater wingspans so they can reach this tree and lay their eggs and have their babies." He looks out the window of the Regency's tenth-floor lounge, as though he might see one of these orange-blue birds flying by.

You follow his gaze, and look out at the smoggy, birdless sky.

"Extreme circumstances require radical change. If you want to survive at least."

"Fascinating," you say.

The bodyguard stands up.

"Did I fail the interview?" you ask.

"Not at all," he says. "I know people. I can tell you're a forthright person, Reeves." You don't know if you want to laugh or cry at this statement, but given that this appears to be the end of the interview, you simply nod.

"Well," says the practical secretary, never one to admire silence for long, "I have a room key."

"Oh, good," you say, as casually as you can muster.

"She's taking over Ivy's room," she explains to the actress. She hands you the key card and tells you your room number at the Grand. You place the key card in the front pocket of your jeans, and push it in deep. You want to make sure there's no chance it could fall out. "Can one of you walk her over?" the pale practical secretary says to the security guards. To you she says: "Maybe you want half an hour to pack your things?"

Your suitcase is already packed and stashed under the massage table in the poolside dressing room.

"That should be enough time," you say.

You take the elevator back to the pool area, and you retrieve your suitcase from under the massage table. You're relieved it's still there. You sit dressed by the pool for twenty-five minutes, and then meet the redheaded bodyguard in the tenth-floor lounge. He takes the handle of the suitcase; it has wheels but he chooses to carry it. You don't check out of the Regency. Instead you just leave. If the hotel ever receives any inquiries about the charge on Sabine Alyse's card, they might remember you as a woman who disapproved of the film crew's attire and was sent champagne.

You walk across the street and into the lobby of the Grand, the bodyguard carrying your suitcase all the while. He leads you up to your room, and opens the door for you.

"Thank you," you say. You want to make sure he leaves. You don't want to talk about evolution anymore.

The room is standard, without the luxuries of the Regency. Outside the window you have a better view of the band shell you could see from your last hotel room. You realize the band shell is part of the Jazzablanca Festival. A jazz trio is playing something experimental, and the stage is surrounded by a small crowd of men in leather jackets and girlfriends holding their arms. Everyone seems unsure of whether they should be dancing, so they slightly sway this way and that. You turn your attention back to the hotel room. Housekeeping has come, so there's no sign of Ivy. You wish you knew something about her. The wastebasket, of course, has been emptied.

Waiting for you on the desk is a large envelope with the name "Reeves Conway" on it.

You shake out the envelope and find a small packet. It seems to be a script, but printed and sized in miniature. It's one-fourth the size of normal pages, as if for a movie being made by tinier people in a tinier, other world.

The top page says: *A Different Door*, which you didn't know until now was the name of the film. A "call time" is listed for each member of the cast and crew. You search for your name. It's not there. You go through it again. Then you see your sister's baby's name is there. Strange, you think. The name you must start recognizing as your own.

"Transportation" will greet you at 7 A.M. outside the Grand and you will be taken to "California, Casablanca." The famous American actress will not be showing up until 2 P.M., and that will be for makeup.

The hotel phone rings as you're flipping through the pages.

It's the secretary to the famous American actress.

"Did you get the sides?"

You have no idea what she's talking about, but glance at the small stapled pages in your left hand.

"Yes?" you say.

"Good."

"So you know you'll be picked up at seven tomorrow."

"Yes, and I'm going to . . . California?"

"Isn't that funny," she says, sounding very serious. "There's an affluent neighborhood in Casablanca called California where the homes are Beverly Hills–big and there are palm trees and all that." She could not sound more bored as she tells you this. "They couldn't find this site until a week ago, but the house is perfect for *A Different Door.*"

After she's hung up, you flip through the small pages that you now know are called sides. It occurs to you that you have no idea what the movie is about apart from what you've observed so far: a young American woman entering a hotel. The sides don't provide much illumination. They tell you that in the first scene that's being filmed the next day the main character, Maria, arrives at Kareem's family home in Casablanca.

You have no idea who Kareem is.

In the scene, Kareem's mother greets Maria and it's a some-what tearful encounter. You can't say for sure but your guess is that Maria and Kareem were dating in America, and now—for reasons that are unclear to you in the small sampling of the script—Kareem is dead. Then Kareem's best friend comes for dinner and there's an attraction between him and Maria that they have to hide from Kareem's mother.

You read the sides twice. You can see why the famous American actress took the part. It's a good role for her, and one that will surprise audiences since she's returning to her more independent-film origins. You once read a film critic's opinion that a film can never be better than the script, but you were never sure if you agreed with that. Which is why it stuck with you. In this case you think the film might end up being better than the script. She's a good actress.

You look out the window of your hotel room, at the plaza below. Tonight's show is ending. People are radiating out in all directions from the central stage. From where you stand, they form a flower, blossoming. A firework, exploding.

Tomorrow you will go to California.

At just before 7 A.M. you stand outside the entrance of the Grand. Your schedule says *7 A.M. Transportation to set:* but you're not sure what "transportation" means—taxi, bus, plane? You see a large white bus with green Arabic letters on it. A man with a silver clipboard stands by the front door and you approach him.

"Are you going to Meknes?" he asks.

"No, I'm going to California?" you say.

He stares at you. "This bus is tour bus going to Meknes twice a week."

"Oh, I'm going to California. Just for today."

"We don't go to California," he says.

You nod as though you knew this, and walk back to the bench in front of the hotel.

A van pulls up and a man with hairy arms and no facial hair comes over and introduces himself as the driver who will be taking you to the set.

He opens the side door of the van and you slide into the first row of seats. He gets back into the driver's seat, but leaves the door open. You sit in silence for a full five minutes.

"Are we waiting for someone else?" you finally ask.

"Yes, two people."

"Oh," you say. You sit in the parked van not knowing exactly what to do with yourself.

You read over the sides again. You study the stage directions in particular. You have memorized your lines, though you know you are probably not expected to. They are not actually your lines. You have to remind yourself of this. Over the course of the night you have begun to think of the Maria character as a hybrid between you and the famous American actress. You imagine her as a third person the two of you have created.

"You must be the new stand-in!" a voice booms. You turn and see a thin Indian man in his early forties stepping into the van.

He introduces himself as a producer on the film and you introduce yourself as your niece.

Another man, an overweight American producer with a goatee and expensive-looking sunglasses, enters the van. He looks like he's twenty-five. After listening to him talk for a minute you think it's likely he actually is twenty-five. You imagine he's recently been able to access his trust fund and is trying to make it in the movie business.

The driver whose name you didn't understand closes the van door. "We are off to California!" he says.

"Not all movies are made in California," the trust funder whispers under his breath.

You consider telling him it's the name of a neighborhood in Casablanca that resembles California but refrain because you don't want to insult him and potentially make an enemy so soon.

"California is the name of a neighborhood in Casablanca," the Indian producer says.

The young American producer is silent, which means he didn't know this. How could he not know this? It's possible he is being used for his money and not being consulted on or informed about decisions.

You must not have disguised your amusement at the Indian producer's comment well enough. The young American producer stares at you with his challenging twenty-five-year-old eyes. "What happened to the other stand-in?" he says to no one in particular. "How come no one told me there was a new stand-in?"

"Didn't you hear about the scandal?" says the Indian producer. He is clearly excited by the use of the word "scandal." "She fell in love with someone."

"On set?" the young American producer says. He's annoyed that he wasn't informed of the affair. No one tells this young man anything.

"What I heard is she flirted with a man who worked at the hotel in Marrakech," the thin Indian producer says. "Now he thinks they are in love and he followed her here to Casablanca. She has to be sent home because she can't focus at work and because her husband is going to divorce her."

"If the husband at home is going to break up with her, she might as well stay here, right?" says the young American producer.

He doesn't wait for a response, but leans forward to direct a pressing question to the driver. "Are we going to be late?"

"Lots of traffic in Casablanca," the driver admits.

"But you know where we're going, right?" says the young American producer.

"Yes, I know the area. The streets in California are not all with signs."

"Fuck me," says the young American producer.

The drive from the hotel to California, according to your schedule, is supposed to take fifteen minutes. In twenty minutes you have moved ten blocks, maybe twelve.

"Why didn't anyone take Casablanca traffic into the equation?" asks the young American producer, of no one in particular. "I grew up in L.A. Everyone always takes traffic into the equation."

He spends the remainder of the drive on his cell phone, making calls to find out how late everyone is, how behind schedule they are with filming. "It's important for me to know this information," he says into the phone more than once.

The thin Indian producer texts silently. You assume his texts are concerned with gossip about the previous stand-in.

The driver of the van is lost. He's stopping every other block to ask locals how to get to where he's going. Looking out the window you see that he's right, no streets seem to have signs.

Finally, the driver finds the street. You know you're in the vicinity because you begin to see large trucks for props and catering and small trailers, as well as many vans identical to the one you're now in. All the houses in the neighborhood are large, and some have guards. It must be one of the times of day when Muslims pray, because the guards are all on the ground, bowing. You wonder if thieves ever take advantage of the times when they're praying.

With its regal, curved stairway at the entrance and large pots filled with bright-colored flowers, the house where the filming is taking place does in fact look like a mansion in Beverly Hills. You haven't seen many other flowers in Casablanca. You enter the house and your presence is barely acknowledged by the crew members, who don't know who you are and yet don't stop you from walking in off the street. They assume anyone who enters has a right to be there.

The rugs have been rolled into logs and pushed to the side of the room and a camera and a dolly have been set up, along with a monitor. You know these are the terms for the devices because a printed-out label has been attached to each piece of equipment, announcing their names in Arabic and English.

A slender woman with a side ponytail and wearing a black jumpsuit is busily removing all the photographs hanging in the living room and replacing them with framed photos of the actors who are supposed to inhabit the house in the film. Through the large back window, you glimpse the yard: a tiled pool, now drained, and a flat, bright green lawn.

It's clear who the owner of the house is. She's in her early fifties, wearing black leather pants, high-heeled boots, and a be-jeweled sweater. She walks around the set snapping photos on her phone, but never gets too close to people, and never takes straight-on photos of the director or the crew. Instead she takes photos of pieces of furniture she could take photos of at any time: the sofa, the dining room table. She appears nervous. She was probably initially flattered her home was selected for the film, but now she seems like the hostess of a party that's been crashed by a hundred more people than expected. She retreats into the kitchen, leaving the door open so she can still observe what's going on. She picks up the phone, presses a number that's been preprogrammed and talks skittishly. You hear her say the famous American actress's name. This seems to calm her down.

You look for a familiar face, for anyone you know who can tell you where to go. The tattooed man spots you and lifts up his chin in recognition. He approaches you and without saying hello he steers you toward the front door. "We should go to the wardrobe trailer," he says.

You walk back outside and pass the young American producer, who's still on the phone. He hasn't entered the house yet, though he spent the entire van ride in an agitated state because he wasn't there.

The tattooed man knocks on a trailer door and a Moroccan woman wearing a black tank top and what looks like a ball gown as a skirt opens the door. She holds a cigarette in her left hand. You recognize her from the night of filming you witnessed.

"This is the new Ivy," he says.

"Hi, new Ivy," she says, and blows smoke up toward the top of the doorframe.

"Come," she says. You step up and she closes the door.

The smell of the smoke in the trailer is immediately dizzying.

She is young, midtwenties, with short curly hair and many earrings.

She scans your body and takes a look at her set of sides. Then she turns to one of her three racks of clothing and rummages through them until she finds what she's looking for: a dark blue dress. It's calf-long and fitted on top without being too tight.

"It's the same thing Maria wears today," she says. "Can you put on?"

"Sure," you say. "Where should I change?"

"Here is good," she says, gesturing to the floor between you. "I turn around," she says, and she does. She is still so close to you, still smoking.

When you've changed you fold your clothes neatly and place them on a chair. Sensing that you're dressed, she turns back around.

"That fits," she says. She seems surprised, and not unhappy. She observes you for a moment. You don't know where to look as she runs her eyes over your body. She puts her cigarette out, and from the top of a dresser removes a pincushion shaped like a tomato. She sticks two pins in her mouth, and continues to speak. "So doesn't go open in front here," she says, and pins the dress together so no cleavage shows. It's an intimate moment but she doesn't seem embarrassed or apologetic. "There," she says.

She stares at you.

"Do you want spank?" she asks.

"Excuse me?" you say.

"Spank. For your stomach."

"Oh, Spanx," you say. You've never worn them. You look at your profile in the mirror. She gives you a pair of Spanx and you inelegantly pull them on because there's no way to easily stretch them over your thighs, your belly.

She hands you a pair of flats. They fit you though she hasn't asked your size.

The door opens and the young Moroccan woman with long black hair and a short apron, with brushes sticking out of its pockets, enters the smoky trailer. The makeup artist.

The smoker and the makeup artist exchange a few words in Arabic. The smoker translates: "She likes put some makeup on you."

"Okay," you say. "I'll do whatever's expected of me."

"It's not necessary for stand-in, but for her it is as a . . . challenge," she tells you.

"A challenge?" you say, implying that her translation is incorrect. But you know it isn't. She's used the exact right word. You applied your new foundation so lightly this morning that it's already worn off. The makeup artist looks at your skin the way hikers look at a mountain, like something she could conquer if she had the chance.

You are seated in front of a mirror in the trailer and then turned away from it. Your hair is brushed back from your face and fastened with a rubber band at the nape of your neck. The makeup artist spends what seems like twenty minutes on your eyelids. She is meticulous in her strokes. You know she, like others before her, is opting for the *distract, distract, distract* approach.

When she's done with your eyelids, you open them and see her looking quizzically at your skin. She shakes a bottle of foundation, and squirts a drop the size of a quarter onto the back of her left hand. Then she applies the foundation with quick, sloppy strokes over your chin, your cheek, your nose, your forehead. Gone are the small, precise strokes she used on your eyelids.

When she's finished she turns you to the mirror. You try not to react. Your skin looks as uneven as tree bark, the makeup emphasizing every ridge, bump, and dip. You thank her profusely, knowing that you will soon be searching for the first available bathroom to wash the makeup off.

While your foundation was being applied the wardrobe woman was brushing a wig. This is the wig you'll be wearing to resemble the famous American actress. The wardrobe woman resecures the rubber band at your nape and bobbypins the stray hairs away from your face. She places the wig over your head.

The color of the wig is shades darker than your own—it's

the dark color your hair appeared to be on the video taken by the surveillance camera at the Golden Tulip. And the length of the hair on the wig is the same length as the actress's. It's the same length your hair was before you cut it to look like Sabine Alyse's passport photo. You are putting on a wig so you more closely resemble the way you looked before you weren't you.

The wig is itchy on your scalp and you raise your hand to scratch your head, and both women almost scream. It's as though you've reached for a knife.

"Do not touch," the wardrobe woman says.

"Okay," you say.

She adjusts the wig's fringe of bangs. The actress has bangs for this movie, so of course the wig has bangs too.

There's a knock at the door. It's the tattooed man. He exchanges a few words with the women and then looks at you. He nods, seemingly satisfied with your transformation, your wig.

You thank the women and exit the trailer and the tattooed man walks you to the house.

"Is there a bathroom I can use?" you ask him.

He walks you to a trailer that has a bathroom. You enter the small bathroom, and immediately wash your face. It looks better without the makeup that's just been applied. There's no towel, so you use toilet paper to dry your skin. Small pieces of the toilet paper stick to your chin, your upper right cheek. You pick the pieces off, toss them in the wastebasket, and rejoin the tattooed man, who's waiting for you outside the trailer.

He walks you into the house and introduces you to the

director. The director is Moroccan, wearing a light brown scarf wrapped around his neck so many times it resembles the bottom half of a beehive. He has an actual director's chair with his name on it. He's squat and commanding and you can see how some women might find him attractive, but you don't.

He seems to be able to discern this as well—the fact that you will not fall for him the way most women do—and so after shaking your hand in a hard and meaningful way, and apologizing for not getting the chance to interview you the way he usually does before filming—he releases your fingers and you begin to fade from his attention.

As an afterthought, he introduces you to two young Moroccan girls, sisters, who will be in the scene with you. They are ten and twelve years old, wide-eyed with long dark hair that falls in curls. The director turns his back on you, the equivalent of walking away to get a drink at a party. He's passing you off.

You like the sisters right away. They tell you they're taking the day off from school, but didn't want to brag to their teachers that they were in a film, so instead they called in sick.

"Your parents must be so excited," you say. "Are they here?"

The girls look at each other and for a moment you envy the communion between happy sisters, the comfort of having someone who is always with you and who knows what you're thinking. When you were young you thought your twinship could be like that; when you were older you thought marriage might be like that. But you were twice mistaken.

"They don't really believe we're in this movie," the younger sister says.

"What do you mean?" you ask.

"We told a lie once," says the older sister with the narrower face.

They wait for you to ask what kind of lie. If you ask, you're positive they won't tell you. You say nothing.

"We said we were in a film with George Clooney and we weren't," one of them says.

"But your parents brought you here, right?" you say.

They shake their heads no, but in different ways. The shorter one is much more exaggerated in her movements.

You tell the girls they're "badasses." You have no idea why you say this or where it comes from. Maybe from spending time with the American actress? You don't think you've ever said "badass" before. The sisters smile. They have no idea what it means.

The girls ask if they can take a picture with you.

"Sure," you say, and the three of you take a photo together with you in the middle. You offer to take a picture of them with the famous American actress when she arrives on set, and their excitement shows in their eyes.

The director whistles. He actually whistles and everyone turns silent. He details what's going to happen in the upcoming scene, and where he wants everyone.

He describes it in Arabic for five minutes and then takes thirty seconds to explain what he's said in English. It's a good thing you've studied your sides so carefully. He shows everyone where they're supposed to stand in the scene. He knows you don't understand, so he puts his hands on your arms and moves you the way a physical therapist might shift your position. You are quickly learning that most of your job is to help with the blocking.

The scene goes like this: Maria enters the room and meets Kareem's nieces, the adorable sisters. Though she's never met them before, she's so overwhelmed by the sight of them and by the memory of Kareem, who's now deceased, that she gets on her knees and hugs them. She tries not to cry. Then she moves over to the dining area. She tries to hug Kareem's mother, but the mother is cold and inaccessible and instead shakes Maria's hand. Maria is taken aback by her demeanor. Kareem's mother then introduces Maria to Kareem's best friend. You, Maria, must shake his hand. But there is clearly an attraction between Maria and the friend. This attraction doesn't escape the notice of Kareem's mother, who throughout the course of the meal behaves in an abrupt and rude manner.

The cameras start rolling, and they move forward and backward on their tracks. The director watches the monitor, his expression indecipherable.

You walk through the part, uttering your lines without forgetting one of them. The young sisters give warm hugs. Kareem's mother is dressed head to toe in black; she's grieving and rude. For a moment you forget it's make-believe and interpret her coldness as a personal affront. When she introduces you to Kareem's best friend, you find him sexy, though two minutes before, when the cameras were off during the run-through, you didn't notice much about him. You wonder if it's the lighting. No, you think, it's the realization that the cameras are on.

You are distracted and forget your line and your stage direction. You were supposed to be seated at the dining room table by now. The director yells a word that you know must mean "Cut!"

"Do you want to talk or should we try again?" he asks.

"Let's try again," you say.

The second time goes well. You move from place to place with ease. As you feel some other rhythm take over your body, you're reminded of diving. You loved diving because your mind could be quiet; your body knew what to do.

You go through the scene a third time and you can feel the magic fading—in part because the cinematographer's experimenting with a new camera movement that's too abrupt, too close, too violating for the actors. The director must sense this too. He asks everyone to return to the way they shot the second take. You know this because just before shooting again, he says to you: "For those of you who don't speak Arabic, we're going back to the before."

Go back to the before, you think to yourself. You know that, in your own life, it's not something you will ever choose to do.

After the fourth take, you're finished with the scene. There are many hours remaining before the famous American actress comes on set. You wait. You watch others move equipment around and eat and look busy. For the first time in your life you wish you smoked and consider accepting a cigarette if someone offers you one. No one offers you one.

The snack bar is inviting. There are large jars of various

colorful candies and a tray of sliced oranges. You place oranges and licorice sticks on a small plate and stand in a corner eating more than you need. You have no one to talk to, no place to retreat to.

Finally, the famous American actress shows up. She greets you hello informally, as though you've barely met. You are saddened for a moment, until you remind yourself that she is going to work, this is serious for her. She can't keep track of everyone's feelings, let alone yours. She is introduced to the sisters, who beam when they shake her hand, and then to the actor playing Kareem's friend, who tries so hard not to be impressed by her that his resistance proves his infatuation.

You watch the famous American actress go through the scene you just rehearsed and you can see all your shortcomings and failures. You were pretending to be Maria; she inhabits Maria. You watch the director do three takes and then say to the famous American actress, "We've got it!"

You are happy for her, happy for the film. You have no right to feel so proprietary after your short period of work but you feel you've played an important part.

The tattooed man yells something in Arabic. Then translates. "Everyone on staff can go have dinner outside in the tent," he tells you.

The crew and the actors are asked to be quiet. You are all reminded this is a residential neighborhood. In the dark you move slowly and clumsily, like cows, down the street to the tent that's been erected at the bottom of the small hill.

Dinner is rice, salad, and stewed vegetables. The meal is

served buffet style and you sit at a table with the woman in charge of props and the woman who is the script supervisor. Both of them are young, both are graduates of a film school in Morocco. The three of you talk for ten minutes in English and then they turn to Arabic. You focus on your food. You did not know there was so much sitting around on film sets, so much waiting.

The next scene involves Maria sitting in bed, reading a book. You return to the trailer, to the cigarette smoke. A long and demure dark blue nightgown has been selected. While you're getting changed the smoking woman in charge of costumes gently reprimands you for not taking off the blue dress before eating dinner. "Next time you take off first," she says.

You wear the nightgown and are directed to a room on the second floor of the house. It's a beautiful room with a canopy bed. Now the owner of the house, the woman in the bejeweled sweater, is taking photos of you. She's smiling and you can see she's become much more comfortable with the shoot. She's invited two friends over: one wears a leopard-print blouse and the other also wears a bejeweled sweater. You try not to think about her. The bejeweled sweater lady's friends take pictures too. You want to tell them you're no one, but the occasion doesn't arise.

You are propped on the bed for a long time while the director and the cinematographer deliberate over how to shoot the scene. The director comes over several times to adjust your body's posture. "Sorry," he says. "To look natural it is a bit uncomfortable." While the director and cinematographer talk and point and adjust the cameras, the prop woman tells you to pick a book from the bookshelf—any book that appeals. You select a book of poetry by Rumi, an English translation. You flip through it until you find a title that appeals to you and you read the poem four times:

THE DIVER'S CLOTHES LYING EMPTY

You're sitting here with us, but you're also out walking
in a field at dawn. You are yourself
the animal we hunt when you come with us on the hunt.
You're in your body like a plant is solid in the ground,
yet you're wind. You're the diver's clothes
lying empty on the beach. You're the fish.

In the ocean are many bright strands
and many dark strands like veins that are seen
when a wing is lifted up.
Your hidden self is blood in those, those veins
that are lute strings that make ocean music,
not the sad edge of surf, but the sound of no shore.

The poem resurrects an image in your mind. The summer you were fifteen you were training as a junior lifeguard. One night an older boy whose parents were out of town had five friends over and your sister drank too many margaritas, took off her clothes, and jumped in the crescent-shaped pool. She was too drunk to swim, and you rescued her. Gave her CPR. How strange it was to have your lips on hers. They were salty from the margaritas, cold from the pool. She made you promise to never tell your parents.

The director and the cinematographer have reached a decision.

"You are done," the director tells you.

"That was it?" you ask.

"Yes."

The movie star is ushered into the bedroom and you are ushered out.

The woman in charge of props follows you. "I need the book," she says, and takes it from your hands. She doesn't know you've earmarked the page of the poem.

It's after 9 P.M. Outside, there is a man with three cell phones. He is the director of transportation. He tells you he'll get you in a van going back to your hotel. You stand there, waiting while he makes more calls. Ten minutes later you and the tired young girls and the young American producer and the Indian producer and two Moroccan members of the crew are directed toward a van.

The driver takes you a few blocks, to the edge of the affluent neighborhood of California, and suddenly it ends. There are large empty dirt lots that will be built upon one day, but now are vacant and frightening. The driver takes a right. Then another right, and another. Soon you have gone around the block and the van is once again facing the dirt lots.

"Do you know where you're going?" the young American producer asks.

"Yes," the driver lies.

It's decided the girls will be driven home first because their house is on the way to the hotel. They know the name of their street but they're unable to give the driver directions.

"It's by the big mosque," they tell him, unhelpfully.

Fifty minutes later you arrive at their house in the dark. Their parents are standing outside, worried, and stare suspiciously at the driver and the van in general. The girls do not say good-bye to you or your fellow passengers, and don't thank the driver for the ride.

You don't realize until the doors close behind them that you're still wearing your wig. You take it off and set in on your lap like a pet.

It takes forty-five more minutes before you're back at your hotel. When the van doors open and you all emerge into the bright lights outside the hotel you see that everyone looks as wrecked as you feel from the drive.

You say good night to each other without really looking at one another, and then realize you all need to take the elevator up to your rooms. So you stand awkwardly in front of the elevators, waiting for one to descend to the lobby. When the bell dings, and the doors open, you all rush inside, as though you can't wait to be enclosed in a small space together again. As each person exits to go to their floor, they are bade good night, in an extra-polite manner to make up for the rushed good nights everyone murmured when they exited the van.

You slide your key card into your lock and the moment you open the door you hear the hotel phone ringing in your room. You run to the phone, allowing the door to slam behind you.

"There you are!" says a voice. You know it's the voice of the famous American actress. You knew her voice before you met her. You once had a conversation with your twin about how actresses today don't have voices that are as recognizable as actresses from classic Hollywood. Katharine Hepburn's voice is a thing of the past. But you cited this famous American actress's voice as an exception. She has a good voice, with a bit of gravel and grit to it.

"Yes, here I am," you say, overly out of breath from your simple dash across the room. "It took us forever to get home."

"Really?" she says. "You should have come with me. I've been back here for over an hour. At least. This is maybe the fifth time I've tried your room."

You ask if anything's wrong.

"Wrong? No, not at all. Oh, I see. Because I called so much. No, I just really wanted to get a drink, and you're the only person I could think of."

"Thank you." You say this flatly, facetiously. You say it like you're talking to an old friend.

"I didn't mean it that way. I mean, I thought you'd be up for a drink and we could talk a little."

You look at the bedside clock: 11:13 P.M.

"Sure. Where do you want to go?"

"Go?" she says. "I can't go anywhere. I already said good night to the guys."

You realize she means her bodyguards.

"Right, of course," you say. There's so much you have to learn.

"But what if you met me in the tenth-floor lounge?"

The Regency. You should never go back there again. There's a chance that by now Sabine Alyse's credit cards have been traced, there's a chance the manager will recognize you.

You remember that you have the wig. "Okay," you say.

"Great. I'll see you in five minutes, Reeves," she says, and before you can say anything else, she hangs up.

You go to the bathroom and put your wig on in front of the mirror. You look exhausted. You are exhausted. Your sides for the next day are on the desk. Your pick-up time the next morning is at 7 A.M. Tomorrow is a complicated day, you've been told: they're shooting a scene outside, in traffic. You vow to yourself to be in bed by midnight. The famous American actress must understand—she has to work tomorrow, too.

You exit your hotel and cross the narrow street to the Regency. You touch your wig and take a deep breath before entering. No one you recognize and no one who would recognize you is in the lobby. You take the elevator to the tenth floor. You remove the wig before the doors open and place it behind a pot that holds a small tree with long fronds, just outside the entrance to the lounge.

The famous American actress is sitting in the lounge wearing flannel pajamas with pastel-colored hippopotamuses all over them. Pink, lavender, and baby-blue hippopotamuses.

"Don't laugh," she instructs you, by way of greeting. "I know they're ridiculous but they're comfortable. My boyfriend never lets me wear them at home, so I have no choice but to wear them here."

You want to say, *You do have a choice to not wear pajamas at all in public since most people don't and that Moroccan bartender there could take a photo of you and it would be all over the Internet in about thirty seconds*, but you refrain. You suddenly have empathy for the pale practical secretary; this actress needs supervision.

The bartender comes over. He's the same one from yesterday. You half expect him to pull out his phone, take a photo, and run away, out of the hotel and into the night and onto the Web.

"What do you want to drink? I'm having a G and T," she says.

"Sounds good. Same. *La même*," you say to the bartender.

"Why'd it take you so long to get back from the set?" the famous American actress asks you.

You explain that the young sisters needed a ride home, and they didn't know directions.

"Their parents weren't on set?" she says.

"I guess not."

"Wow," she says. "That's amazing. When I was young, my dad was there at every film I shot."

"The girls told me their parents didn't really believe they were in a movie with you."

"I posed with them, so I guess they'll have some proof. Sweet girls. Wonder if they'll make it."

Your drinks arrive quickly, as though they were made before you ordered. You consider that is a possibility.

You tell the famous American actress you think it might be hard for them to make it in Morocco.

"I thought that before I came," she says, and sips her

drink through a small black straw, "but do you know what I found out?"

"No," you say.

"There's a huge film school in Morocco! And guess who supports it?"

You tell her you have heard about the school, but you don't know who supports it.

"You don't know?"

You shake your head.

"All these big names. Martin Scorsese and people like that helped start it or they fund it or something like that."

You say wow.

"Wow is right," she says. "That's why they can film *A Different Door* here. They have such a great Moroccan crew. That was half the reason they were able to shoot it here—they didn't have to bring hardly fucking anybody over. Except for me, my secretary, the bodyguards, and Ivy, my stand-in who abandoned me."

"I heard she fell in love with someone who worked at the hotel in Marrakech." You feel the gin and tonic going to your head.

"At the hotel in Marrakech? You think she fell in love with someone there?" She cackles.

Again: the bizarre laugh.

Again: the question you don't know how to answer. "That's what the producers in the van were talking about," you say.

"She fell in love with the fucking director! Who's fucking married! And *she's* fucking married!"

"Shit," you say, and this amuses her.

"Fucking shit is right," she says. Then she summons the bartender and orders two more gin and tonics. You consider stopping her, reminding her that you have to go to sleep soon and she probably does too. But the truth is you are enjoying all this—the tenth-floor lounge, the drinks, the conversation. When you're with the actress, the life you left at home seems unreal, almost as though the events of the last few months didn't happen.

"So, anyway," she says, after the bartender leaves, "thank God you were here. Because Ivy, who I will admit could be a bit dramatic . . . well, she had to go. I'm sure if she recovers she'll be able to work with me again. She's been my stand-in on, like, nine or ten movies now. She's trying to act, and has had small parts. Nice girl, pretty girl. So tell me about you," the famous American actress says, as though she's exhausted talking about Ivy. "What's your story?"

You laugh nervously. You sound like someone else.

"What's the story of why you're here?" she continues. "Why the fuck are you in Morocco?" She suddenly looks very drunk.

"I left my husband and I wanted to get away."

"A spa day wasn't enough?" She laughs at her own joke.

"I don't ever think I've ever done a spa day, but no, not enough for what he did."

"You should see your face right now. You look like you've been injected with venom or something."

"That's how I feel about my marriage," you say.

"So you came to Casablanca of all places?"

You nod. "Even here didn't seem far enough away." The alcohol is making you more honest than you want to be in her presence.

"And you were just going to stay in Casablanca until . . . until you were offered a role as a stand-in for a movie?"

You tell her about your backpack being stolen at the Golden Tulip.

"Tell me the whole story," she says, and genuinely seems to want to hear it.

You tell her all about the Golden Tulip, about the backpack, the embassy, and Sabine Alyse, how the police asked for your grandfather's name. You haven't talked this much in a week. When you're done recounting the events of the last few days, she shakes her head. This is the response you want. You're afraid of the cackling.

"Holy shit," she says. "Well, that explains the clothes."

You look down at your outfit. "No, my suitcase wasn't stolen. These are the same clothes I owned before."

She sips her drink. She looks as though she's debating whether to apologize. "So is Reeves Conway your real name?"

You tell her it's your sister's baby's name.

"Reeves Conway is your niece?"

"Yes, she's my twin's baby."

"Fucking A. What kind of bodyguards do I have?" She looks up to the ceiling. "I mean they didn't even check you out to see if you were who you said you were."

You tell her that the bodyguard who interviewed you trusted you because you bonded over turtles and birds.

"And that makes you trustworthy? I should fucking have you fired right fucking now. You're an impostor."

You panic. You went too far. Now you're going to be fired, and you have nothing. You should never have been flattered by her invitation for a drink. Especially when she herself said you were the only person she could think of.

A cool sweat runs down your back and collects at the weak elastic band of your underwear.

"I'm sorry," you say.

"I'm sorry too," she says, and her face changes. "I was just fucking with you!"

"Fuck," you say. You don't typically swear but it's contagious and you feel relieved.

She laughs her strange cackling laugh that you now know must be dubbed over if she ever laughs in a film.

"You know I trained as a stage actress, right?" she says. "I really do have some good acting chops. Do you believe me?"

"I have witnessed them firsthand," you say. You wonder what they did when she was a stage actress and they couldn't dub her laugh. Maybe she was only given very serious roles. You understand why she's no longer in theater. You wonder if she does too. Someone must have surely told her about her cackle. But if so, why does she still laugh that way?

"So what is your name?" she says. "Wait!" She extends her hand as though to stop you. "I'm going to try to figure it out."

"Okay," you say.

"Rebecca?"

"No."

"Sybil?"

"No."

"Okay. Give me time. Even one week. I'll get it. Are you staying for the whole shoot?"

"I think so."

"You have nowhere to go? No one expecting you at home?"

You tell her that no one expects you back for another week.

"Does your sister care that you're going around using her daughter's name?"

You tell her your sister doesn't know.

You look at your watch. It's after midnight. You have to get to bed. Maybe it's the gin and tonics that are making you paranoid, but you're getting the strange feeling that the famous American actress wants something from you, that her extending of friendship toward you is calculated. When your sister was most effusive in her kindness toward you, it was because she needed something.

"The call sheet says we're being picked up at seven," you say.

"*You're* being picked up at seven," the famous American actress says. "I don't have to do anything until nine. We're having more drinks."

She pauses to look up. "Garçon," she says, waving the bartender over once again. "I had to play a girl in a French café once," she explains to you. " 'Garçon' was the only word I had to say in the whole fucking movie."

At seven the next morning you and the two producers are picked up and driven through Casablanca's standard morning gridlock to get to the film set. Today's scene takes place in a traffic jam. Given your experience of the city at rush hour, or at any hour, you would think that would mean they could film on any street in Casablanca. What's the need for a set? But the producers inform you that today's shoot is extremely complicated, as they have had to block off two streets and create their own traffic jam. This has entailed obtaining permits from the city, and locating fifty-three period cars from the 1960s. It has also required making sure that the fifty-two extras who have been hired to drive the period cars have insurance, and that they have been background-checked and fingerprinted in the event that they should wish to drive off.

The driver of the fifty-third car, the one who will be chauffeuring Maria, played by the famous American actress, is an actor himself. As you sit in the van with the producers, stuck in real traffic making your way to the manufactured traffic, a situation has arisen. This is what you, in your brief career as a stand-in, have already learned is terminology for a problem. *A situation has arisen.* You imagine that when it was discovered your predecessor, Ivy, was having an affair with the director, and had to go home to face her husband, the same phrase was used to prepare the practical secretary for the debacle ahead: *a situation has arisen.*

The producers panic when they receive the simultaneous texts stating that a situation has arisen. They both jump on the phone. By the time they're off their respective phone calls, the van has traveled half a city block.

"Fuck me," says the young American producer.

"What's wrong?" you ask.

"Maria's chauffeur—the dude who was supposed to play Maria's chauffeur today—doesn't have a driver's license," the young American producer says.

You think of suggesting that someone else play the part of the chauffeur, but you're sure they have already considered this.

"Is it such a problem since he's just going to be sitting in traffic anyway?" you say. "I mean, that's what the sides say. That they're just sitting in traffic, not moving, right?" You take out the sides and read the description aloud: " 'Maria sits in the back of a taxi. She sits there until she gets fed up with the standstill, opens the back door, and marches out onto the street. The cars honk as she walks past.' " You look up from the script. "He doesn't need a driver's license. He won't be moving."

The producers look at each other and nod, then send texts.

You arrive at the makeup trailer. Today the wardrobe woman is inexplicably dressed in Elizabethan attire. You don't comment, you don't ask questions. She is, after all, in charge of costumes. You imagine she's collected several in her career, and keeps them in steady rotation.

"You want the spank again, yes?" she says to you.

You have learned that some things that are phrased as questions are not questions. Yes, you tell her, you want the spank.

There's a knock on the trailer door and you finish hiking up your Spanx, which still takes a bit of effort. When you're dressed the wardrobe woman unlocks the door. You're touched by this small act of courtesy: she locks the door while you change.

The tattooed man steps up into the trailer.

"How are you?" he says, but doesn't wait for a response. He informs you that something different will happen today: you will actually appear in the film.

"What?" you say. You are not excited about this proposition. You think of your twin. You know that if she were in your situation and had just received this news, she would be thrilled. She would be texting her friends, calling your mother. She always likes to brag to your mother, and maybe because of this tendency, you've always felt your mother loves you more. But you can't be certain. Lately, you've been tempted to tell your mother about the details surrounding your recent falling-out with your sister, but you refrained. You even contemplated that instead of flying to Morocco, you would fly to Arizona to visit your mother and her new husband in the large stairless white house they live in on a mesa, but decided against it: you were concerned that if you revealed everything to your mother and she still spoke to your sister, your heart would be broken once more.

The tattooed man has ignored your "What?" and has been speaking Arabic with the wardrobe woman and the makeup woman. Today the makeup woman has a David Bowie–like triangle of eye shadow around her right eye.

When the tattooed man is finished talking with the Elizabethan and David Bowie, he returns his attention to you and your question. He explains that the shots that are filmed from very far away—the scenes that are used to show Maria stuck in traffic—will in fact be the scenes with you in the car. You will be wearing the wig and a scarf around your face, so it's easy enough for them to do a profile shot of you from a distance, sitting in the car.

You pause and agree—you have no choice but to agree—but ask why they don't just use the famous American actress for those shots.

"It's important that she not get exhausted and we have reports that she is getting exhausted."

"Of course," you say. You don't offer that one way for her to conserve energy might be to refrain from drinking gin and tonics until one in the morning. You don't offer that you yourself are exhausted because of her.

The tattooed man and the makeup woman are discussing specifics. They are studying your skin. The wardrobe woman takes a scarf and wraps it around your face. She's demonstrating how much of your face will be covered.

The tattooed man wants to make sure that even if you're shot from a distance, your acne scars will not show. You imagine he's telling the Elizabethan and David Bowie how terrible it would be if viewers thought that the famous American actress had your skin. The three of them stare at you. You're at a loss; you force a smile. Apparently, you're not applying the foundation you bought at the Casablanca beauty store correctly.

The makeup woman gets out her apron with all her brushes, but instead of tying it around her waist, she places it on your lap as though to suggest it's your weight to bear. She spends a good twenty-five minutes layering foundation on your skin. You are turned away from the mirror, which is a good thing. You are afraid of the craterlike quality your skin will take on when she is done. For a moment you feel like contacting the man at the Casablanca beauty store. If only you had saved his card. He could help this woman do her job.

When your face has been slathered in foundation and powders, the wardrobe woman takes a scarf and wraps it around your head. Unsatisfied with the result, she removes it and wraps it once more. The three of them, the Elizabethan, David Bowie, and the tattooed man, discuss your appearance while only occasionally glancing at you. Then phones are removed and photos are taken.

"This is so we can make sure the scarf falls the same way on her," the tattooed man says.

You don't need to ask who *her* is. You know that he means the famous American actress.

The tattooed man escorts you through real Casablanca traffic, until you turn the corner and arrive at the traffic that's been manufactured for the film. Of course the trailers couldn't be on this street—they would be too conspicuous in the shots. Filming has not yet commenced and so the sidewalks are still open to the public. The pedestrians yell at the parked cars, and in particular, at one extra who, for some reason—perhaps he's getting into character—won't stop honking.

It's still morning but you can feel the heat of the day seething up through the cement. This day is hotter than the preceding ones. The old cars are diesel, the smell of their exhaust potent.

The tattooed man walks you to a white car in the middle of all the others. You slide inside the backseat, and greet the driver, who, you know from the *situation that has arisen* with the producers, cannot drive. The tattooed man closes the door. You note the old car has ashtrays, and that it's without seat belts. The upholstery on the backseat bench is leather, cracked. You run your fingers over the ocher stuffing that's trying to emerge.

There's a speaker in the car through which the director is talking. He speaks for five minutes in Arabic, and then translates for you with one sentence: "We start filming in two minutes."

In twenty minutes an announcement comes through the speaker saying the filming is commencing. You sit up tall, looking forward intently. Maria is supposed to be growing increasingly frustrated with the traffic. Your driver has been instructed to honk, joining in on the cacophony being created by the other cars around yours. The horns of old cars sound cartoonish, like horns on bumper cars at an amusement park.

Despite the incessant honking, as you sit in the backseat of a period car in a constructed traffic jam in the heart of Casablanca, you begin to feel something that approximates joy. The film will come out, and though no one will know that you were in the backseat of this car, that you are the one whose scarfed profiled appears in the distance, you will know. You will have existed. You will have proof that you were here.

You are picturing yourself at seventy, looking back on your youth. You will remember that you were young once, that you were thirty-three. You were in a movie in Casablanca. Now that you are on the cusp of being a full-fledged adult, as you now see adulthood, your youth has been documented. Your youth will not be defined by the events of the last several months.

An announcement comes on the speaker and the honking ceases. Twenty minutes later, filming commences again. The cars honk, you sit up straight and look forward intently.

Two hours pass, during which filming occurs five more times. The wardrobe woman comes to the car to rearrange your scarf. She consults the photo on her phone.

You sit for another hour, two hours, three. You try not to think of anything at all.

Then, almost too soon, the famous American actress is escorted under an enormous silver umbrella—the sun is hot—toward the car. The door is opened and you greet her hello. You switch places with her. She slides onto the leather red bench of the backseat.

"Ouch," she says. "The seat is cracked."

You head to the food trailer (they can't have the food outside today, due to the traffic, and the pedestrians who might graze). You eat licorice, olives, cheese, crackers, and slices of salami. The salami here is larger, but cut thinner, like ham. You wait to see if you are needed again.

You are needed one more time, when the actress's makeup needs to be reapplied. The temperature in the car is rising as the day progresses and her mascara is clumping, her lipstick fading as her lips grow increasingly chapped. You return to the car.

"Hello," you say to the driver.

He grunts in return.

The director approaches.

The director asks you to help him block the scene in which Maria exits the vehicle—that's his word, "vehicle"—in a storm of rage so they can get the cameras set up right. You are to open the door, slam it, and walk through the traffic.

You do this three times.

Then the famous American actress returns to the car, her forehead dabbed, her lipstick reapplied and outlined with a red makeup pencil.

It's her turn.

You walk through the fake traffic and back to the food trailer. Even you, who knows better, can't seem to forget the traffic isn't real. You signal to every driver to stop, to not drive; with your hands and your eyes you implore them to not run you over.

You spend the remainder of the day waiting. You eat more olives, more licorice. You chew on mints to cleanse your breath (you're too impatient to slowly let them dissolve in your mouth). Your services might be needed at any minute, you tell yourself. But you are not needed for the rest of the day.

The sadness of being unuseful, which is a particular type of sadness, begins to vine through your body. By 7 P.M. you are wondering if you can take off your wig, scratch your scalp. You have already consumed too many rolls; you were instructed to not eat the sauce-laden dishes offered at the dinner buffet in case you spilled on your outfit, your scarf.

Another two hours pass. The famous American actress comes to the food trailer.

"Hey," you say, surprised that filming, which has gone so slowly, has ended so suddenly.

"Hey," she says. "I'm starving." She picks up a submarine sandwich and bites into it and a slice of tomato slips onto her scarf. She pays it no attention. "This tastes terrible," she says, and places it back down on the tray with the other sandwiches.

"Are you going back to the hotel?" you ask.

"No," she says. "There's this music festival going on—Jazzablanca. Get it?" she says. "My friend Patti Smith is playing." You're tempted to say, *You're friends with Patti Smith?* Instead you say: "She's considered jazz?"

"It's just the name of the festival," she explains. "Anyway, you want to come to the show?"

You shrug only because you're too excited to speak.

The famous American actress opens the jar of M&M's. She doesn't use the silver serving spoon but instead she grabs a handful and pours them into her mouth.

You get a ride to the concert in the famous American actress's van. She has a van and a driver assigned just to her. You sit next to her in the first row of seats. One bodyguard sits in the passenger seat of the van, the other in the row behind you.

The driver has difficulty finding the venue. It's not a normal concert pavilion, but the grandstand of a racetrack that they've closed up with tenting. This is your experience of Casablanca thus far: no one can find the address they're looking for. Most places that are not hotels are identified only by landmarks. The horse track has been described to the driver as exactly that, "the horse track." It doesn't help matters that the driver has been traveling with the film and is from Fez. This is his first week in Casablanca.

Finally, you arrive at the racetrack. One bodyguard gets out of the car, followed by the famous American actress, and the other bodyguard is close behind. You're the last out and you slide the heavy van door shut behind you. Cheers are erupting from inside the tent; the concert is beginning. Two people from the festival are waiting for the famous American actress at the now empty will-call line. She walks up to them and they escort her, you, and the two bodyguards into the makeshift theater.

The stands in the back are filled with people and in front of the stage chairs have been set up in rows, the way they would be in a high school auditorium.

The actress, the bodyguards, and you are escorted to your reserved seats six rows back from the stage. You always wondered who the assholes were who came late to a concert and took up a whole row near the stage, and now you know.

You get into the chairs without drawing attention. Everyone's focused on Patti Smith.

Patti stands on a stage with a neon sign that says JAZZA-BLANCA behind her. She's talking to the audience about how she's always wanted to perform in Morocco because of the desert and because of Moroccan mint tea. She holds up her cup, which ostensibly is filled with Moroccan mint tea, and the audience cheers loudly. Very loudly. They love her.

The actress whispers to you: "If I have to leave early, can you please go backstage after and say hello to Patti for me? Let her know I was here?"

"Okay," you promise, wondering why she'd have to leave early.

You smell expensive perfume, and this is also when you notice the fur. All the women in the rows in front of you are wearing fur. They're extremely dressed up for a rock concert. Some of the women are with men, all of whom are wearing ties, but the majority of women have come in groups with other women. They have coiffed hair and well-applied makeup, and are blessed with either good genes or the funds to improve upon them. None of the women wear hijabs. This is the upper crust of Casablanca. You observe that your group might be the only Westerners in the audience.

Onstage Patti Smith is wearing faded baggy blue jeans, a white blouse, and a man's blazer. Her gray hair is long and parted in the middle. She wears no makeup. She introduces a guitarist and a bassist, and the crowd claps politely.

She sings a cover of Lou Reed's "A Perfect Day" and the crowd goes crazy. Especially the women. The women of Morocco love Patti Smith.

When she sings "Because the Night" everyone around you sings the lyrics too.

> *Come on now try and understand*
> *The way I feel when I'm in your hands*
> *Take my hand come undercover*
> *They can't hurt you now,*
> *Can't hurt you now, can't hurt you now*
> *Because the night belongs to lovers*

Because the night belongs to lust
Because the night belongs to lovers

You're unable to keep your eyes on the performance because you're focused on the women around you. They know every word, and sing along, joining Patti in proclaiming the night belongs to them, the lovers, the women who lust.

Everyone is up on his or her feet except one woman sitting in front of you. She doesn't want to stand. Every thirty seconds or so, her furred friends try to get her to join them, and she refuses. You notice that the bodyguards have their eyes on her, on this woman who won't get up on her feet at a Patti Smith concert. Her refusal to stand makes her intriguing to the bodyguards.

When Patti Smith sings "People Have the Power," the crowd is raucous. Even the reluctant stander in front of you finally raises herself to her feet and you sense the bodyguards relaxing.

But then a sound startles you—it's the sound of trampling, like horses stampeding. You turn around to see if the audience members in the back are dancing so intensely that the stands are collapsing. Everyone near the stage begins turning around. And then the audience starts to collectively look up. You follow their gaze and see what they see—it's raining. Torrential rain. The downpour sounds like rocks avalanching onto the tent, and it seems likely that the rain might succeed in bringing down the tent on top of everyone inside.

You turn back to the stage and see that Patti Smith and Lenny Kaye and Tony Shanahan look confused; they have no idea why the front rows of the audience have turned around.

They keep playing, but you feel you're seeing them without their performance faces on. They seem baffled, concerned. It's then that one of the furred women two rows ahead, who is looking back to observe the center of the tent, catches a good look at the famous American actress. The furred woman does a double take to be certain, and then tells her friend standing next to her. The friend turns around to stare, and then says something to the friend standing next to her. Within a matter of seconds you start to hear the famous American actress's name being spoken. Then it's not spoken but being called out. They're calling out her first name as though she's a friend they haven't seen for a while. They want to see if she turns and looks in their direction. If she responds to the name they'll know it's her.

Suddenly, a collective gasp erupts behind you. You turn to see what's happening. The rain breaks though the tent. The power goes out. But Patti Smith and her guitarist and bassist don't stop. They continue singing a cappella:

> *I believe everything we dream*
> *Can come to pass through our union*
> *We can turn the world around*
> *We can turn the earth's revolution*
> *We have the power*
> *People have the power . . .*

The crowd grows crazier than before. The rain is hitting the floor and you can feel the vibration of stomping feet. The energy of the crowd has swarmed and collected and is harnessed toward the stage. You are certain the performers can feel this focused beam of energy too because they're singing louder and no longer look at all confused, but the opposite: they have intention. Everyone is singing now about *the power to dream, to rule, to wrestle the earth from fools*. You know this is the reason many people come to concerts, come to witness anything live. There exists the possibility of surprise, of power outages, of connection and communion, the possibility of people who have never before met singing the same song to each other about the power they have to change the world.

You look to your right to see if the famous American actress is enjoying the concert as much as you are. But she's not there. You look to your left. She's not there. In the midst of the chaos, the famous American actress and her two bodyguards have vanished.

You are by yourself for the remainder of the show. The women in front of you who recognized the famous American actress now turn to look at you with disapproving, judgmental eyes, as though you're the one who drove her away.

When the show ends you wait for the crowd to clear out and then head toward the stage. A security guard stands before a staircase, monitoring backstage access. You explain the situation. You tell him where you were sitting. You tell him you were with the actress.

He has three conversations via walkie-talkie. Then you are patted down and allowed backstage. You are given a silver sticker that looks like a sheriff's badge and told you must wear it on your shirt. The security person walks you to the green room, which is up a set of stairs. As you climb the stairs you hear laughter. It's only as you get closer to the laughter that you realize the "green room" is in fact the changing area for jockeys.

Approximately fifteen people are gathered around Patti Smith and her band. You did not know the backstage crowd would be so small. Plates of vegetables and hummus and cakes are arranged on a table. Enough food to feed sixty.

"Hello!" a man says from a distance, and as he approaches he frowns. "Sorry, I thought you were someone else." He puts on his glasses as though to explain his mistake.

"It's okay," you say. "I'm with her. I mean, I was with her, but she had to leave."

"Great," the man says, removing his glasses. He seems relieved to not have to wear them. "Have you met Patti?"

The man who hasn't yet introduced himself to you introduces you to Patti Smith. You shake her hand. You watch your hand being shaken by Patti Smith. You have grown accustomed to the actress's elaborately manicured hands; in contrast, Patti Smith's hands with their short unpolished nails are clearly those of a serious musician.

You tell Patti Smith the actress had to leave and she tilts her head ever so slightly and says she understands, that you never know with crowds.

You are introduced to other people—men who worked with Patti in various countries, and their girlfriends, who are taller than the men and are wearing low-cut shirts. One wears a bustier with a suit jacket over it. She is bursting from it and you try not to stare. You can see that everyone is trying not to stare.

You are the first to dip into the hummus, the only one to eat the shallow glazed cake, topped with an array of orange fruit. When you feel you have stayed too long, you walk to the exit and turn and give a small wave. Everyone returns your polite wave with a more enthusiastic one. You try to interpret this as a good sign—they enjoyed meeting you—and not as a sign that they're relieved by your departure.

The next day, shooting starts at 9 A.M. You are reeling from the night before, and wake up at 7:30, earlier than you wanted to. You decide to swim laps. The pool at the Grand is smaller than the pool at the Regency, its shape more traditional. You dive in.

You've swum twenty laps when you see the famous American actress approaching, flanked by her bodyguards. It's 8 A.M. You swim underwater to the other side of the pool. When you lift your head, the three of them are standing there before you.

"Can I talk to you for a minute?" the famous American actress says.

You have the feeling you're in trouble but don't know why.

"In private," she says to the bodyguards. "We'll be over there." She points to two chaise longues out of the forty facing the pool. All are vacant.

You hoist yourself up out of the water. The two men look at you for one second too long. You grab your towel and wrap it around your waist.

The famous American actress sits at the foot of a chaise

longue, and you sit down at the foot of the one next to hers.

"Look at them," she says, staring at the bodyguards. One is three chaise longues to your left, the other four to your right. They are both looking in opposite directions, waiting, watching. There's no one else in the pool area.

"I guess they got frightened last night," you say. Then you add: "That was scary."

"You consider that scary?" she says. "You don't know how it usually is in like L.A. or London or something. Last night was tame. I think the boys just got excited because before coming here we were in the desert for a month. There was no one around us for miles and they had nothing to do."

"It was a little weird how fast it happened," you say, taking another towel from the chaise longue you're sitting on and placing it on your lap like a blanket. Like an elderly lady who gets cold in her living room.

"It's always like that. One person spots you and then suddenly you see, like, a ton of heads turning your direction and—*bam*—it's time to get out of there. Anyway, how was backstage? Did you get a chance to say hi to Patti for me? Tell her I was there?"

"Yeah. I can't believe I was talking to her. She said she understood and she was glad you came."

"Good. Thank you for doing that. I didn't want her to think I was a no-show."

You tell her it was an honor to meet Patti Smith.

The famous American actress looks at you for a moment and then gives you her famous lopsided smile. "You crack me up. You use words like 'honor' and stuff."

"It *was* an honor."

"You're too much," she says.

You look at her and see her brain is already miles away, thinking. You've come to learn something about her that she tries to hide: her mind never rests.

"What are you doing tonight?" she asks.

"I have to work till seven or so. Which means you're probably working later . . ."

"Yeah, I work late tonight."

She looks at the pool, as though considering diving in. "I was wondering if I could ask you a favor."

You shrug, but she's not looking at you—she's still staring at the pool—so you say, "Sure."

"I'm wondering if you'll go out with someone tonight. I'm supposed to meet him for dinner at eight, but I have to work, and things are complicated . . ."

"Who is he?"

"It's a long story," she says, and sighs. "I was sort of dating this man . . . he's a little older, Russian, debonair really, except for some of the bars he took me to in Moscow. Which were really fun, by the way. Bars in Moscow are amazing. Everyone gets naked onstage. Anyway, it was casual but then he fell for me pretty hard and . . ." She doesn't finish the sentence.

"So you want me to go have dinner with him and break up with him for you?" You laugh a little laugh.

"No, no, no . . . the thing is he didn't really fall hard for me, personally. He just fell for the *idea* of me."

"He fell for the idea of dating an actress?"

"Not even that," she says, examining her pedicure. "He

just fell for the idea of youth. Of a young woman listening to everything he said."

"How long were you . . . ?"

"I didn't date him for that long. We'd see each other in different cities. Have dinner, that sort of thing."

"That sounds serious," you say. "It must have taken some effort."

"It wasn't that serious," she says, and you sense she's lying.

"Is he an actor?"

"God no. He's a Russian businessman. A really successful one, actually. Like *really* successful."

"So he's in Casablanca for business?"

"No, no. He came to have dinner with me."

"And you're going to stand him up?"

She sighs as though you're to blame for the situation she's in.

"I don't feel like it. I know he's seen pictures of me with other people recently and I know he's going to be pissed and I'm just not up for it. I think he'll be just as happy to see you."

You tell her there's very little chance he'll be excited to see you if he's expecting her.

"He might be upset for, like, five minutes," she says. "Tops. Then he'll be happy to have a young woman to talk to."

You look at the sky. You look at the pool.

"I don't think I can do it," you say.

"I think you can," she says.

"I don't know."

"I think you can, Reeves, or whatever your real name is."

You look at her, but she's lying flat on the chaise longue now, staring at the hotel as though its profile is interesting.

She's threatening you, you're sure, but she doesn't look threatening. She is brilliant. You're confused. You start to sweat.

"Okay," you say. "I'll do it."

"Really?" she says, sitting up now. She acts as though you're doing her a favor. She's acting as though there's no way in the world she could have implied she would turn you in if you didn't agree. And she's so convincing that for a moment you think you might have imagined that she would blackmail you.

"Promise you'll make sure to show him a good time?"

You wonder what this means. "My clothes are staying on," you say.

"Of course they are," she says in a slightly reprimanding tone. "The car will be here at seven thirty. Just give him my regards and say I'm so sorry I got caught working late."

She stands to leave.

"What's his name?" you call out after her.

"Leopoldi," she says.

You watch her and the bodyguards as they reenter the building. The Moroccan sky above you is pale blue and cloudless, like the sky in a musical production for children.

When you return to your room, you find a green silk dress on your bed. It's lying flat with one sleeve down and the other raised up, as though holding a glass and making a toast. You shouldn't be surprised she already has a dress picked out and has sent it to your room. It was most likely already lying here on your bed even before she approached you at the pool. It's 8:30 A.M. You have to get to the van.

You shower and dress for the day on set. It's a relatively simple shoot compared to yesterday's scene in traffic. In today's scene Maria enters a mosque to pray for Kareem, but she's uncertain about how to position herself. At first she's on her knees with her palms pushed together the way she readied herself for prayer during her Catholic childhood. Once situated, she furtively glances around and sees the Moroccan women are on their knees, but seated back on their heels. Their eyes are closed and their palms extended, as though holding open a book. Maria ends up sitting the way the women around her are sitting, and praying the way they are praying. She prays until she starts sobbing.

There are no lines in today's scenes. The script supervisor has warned you that the director is very indecisive about today's shoot; much of it will be improvised on the spot. So much of it will depend on how well the famous American actress can pull off the scene. There are tears involved: a risky proposition. The famous American actress was criticized for the last film in which she cried. It was an ill-advised romantic comedy set in Rome. Her chin quivered melodramatically. You have a vague recollection of a spoof of her crying scene on *Saturday Night Live*. But then your memory becomes clearer and you remember she was *in* that spoof; she went on *Saturday Night Live* to make fun of herself. And it worked to her advantage; the public forgave her, the public loved her for mocking her own performance. She has good PR people, the American actress does.

You wonder for a moment if it's the PR people who have instructed her not to go on the date tonight. Maybe her cancellation on the businessman has little to do with her level of affection for him, and more to do with how it will look to anyone who sees them on a date and documents the sighting. Photos of her and the current young boyfriend on a sailboat named the *Ooh La La* have been prevalent in the weekly magazines as of late. One headline said: YO HO HO ON THE *OOH LA LA*!

You descend to the lobby and exit the hotel and step into the van, where the Indian producer and the twenty-five-year-old are already seated, waiting for you. You don't know how you fell a few minutes behind. You blame the actress, and mention that she needed to talk to you about something important.

"Is she nervous about the scene today?" the Indian producer asks.

"No," you say, and because you've already learned that he likes scandal, he likes gossip, you reiterate it. "No, she's not at all nervous."

"*I'm* nervous about the crying scene," says the young American producer. "If it were up to me, she would *not* be shown crying. Not after what happened in that ridiculous Italian rom-com fiasco."

You think he has a point, but you can't say anything. You can't betray her. This is the unwritten contract between the talent and the stand-in. Or at least in your case.

You arrive at the mosque and you think you hear yourself inhale sharply. Or maybe it's the three of you—the Indian producer, the twenty-five-year-old, and you—who are collectively caught off guard at the same time. The mosque is enormous, and situated on the water—at first you think it's on its own island. It's white and turquoise with an intricately tiled minaret topped with a gold point as firm and narrow as the needle of a compass. There's a short line of tourists waiting to get into the mosque. You've been told it's one of the only Moroccan mosques that allows non-Muslims to enter.

The van pulls up to one of the trailers parked outside the mosque and the costume department outfits you in a long skirt and a long-sleeved blouse, and the wig. You are given a scarf to place around your hair. No shots of you in the distance will be filmed today, so they let you arrange the scarf yourself.

From the side of the mosque you see a series of double doors in the shape of pointed arches and framed by columns. Some of the doors are clad in bronze. The film crew enters through one of the bronze-clad doors and is escorted up to a room on the second floor.

The stairway itself has multiple arches and decorative woodcarving. You are told that they lead to the Women's Gallery, which is hidden from view from the enormous prayer hall below. When you enter the Women's Gallery you are overcome by the size of the room—it could easily fit five thousand women. Chandeliers hang in a row down the center of the room, between a series of high scalloped archways. The floors are tiled, keeping the temperature of the room cool.

The film crew takes half an hour to set up their equipment. The director paces, looking apprehensive about this scene. He holds his head between his hands as though to suggest the vise grip on his brain.

The extras are Moroccan women of all ages, wearing

clothes appropriate for a mosque. You watch as they store their shoes in the small shoe compartments that have been built into the prayer rugs and kneel toward Mecca. You wonder if they are actually using this time to pray.

The director calls you over and instructs you to enter this room of the mosque as though in awe. This is not difficult. You enter the room and admire the architecture. You walk over to where the women are praying. You remove your shoes and store them in the prayer rug's compartments. You adjust your scarf around your head, making sure you're more than adequately covered, and sit back on your heels. You assume the same position as the women around you.

One of the younger extras is carrying a baby in a sling. You cannot see the baby's face, but still you stare.

As you relax on your heels in the mosque you are thinking of your sister's nine-week-old baby. Your niece.

You think of your sister, of how she invited you over to her home that early spring morning, over a year ago now, when the flowers in her garden were the colors of Easter. You sat on her deck, in matching deck chairs with red pin-striped cushions. She worked an as interior designer and had directed immeasurable attention toward the purchase of everything in her home. She turned toward you and cried as she told you that after five years of miscarriages, it was definitive: she and her husband, Drew, had resigned themselves to the fact that they would not be parents. All she ever wanted was a child, she told you. "I just know it's because of that hatchet job of an abortion I had my senior year." Of course you remembered it: you had told her you couldn't drive her to the clinic because you were meeting with a recruiting coach, but it was a lie. You were tried of always bailing her out of trouble. Your sister drove herself, and for this, you have always felt terrible.

She moved herself to your deck chair and positioned herself so she could literally cry on your shoulder—which you also now realize was part of her dramatic ploy. At the time you fell for it, though: you offered to help her however you could.

She lifted her head from your shoulder and said, "Really?"

Later you would think about how quickly she said this. Later, the alacrity of her response would make you question whether her crying was calculated, would make you wonder if she had been manipulating you all along. Her relationships were as well choreographed as her home—no vase had been set down temporarily on a table, no throw pillow was accidental in color, no rug was a square inch too big or small. She designed and selected everything according to her specifications. On this particular Sunday morning she sought your pity, she wanted you to sacrifice your body for her needs. She preyed upon the fact that you had always wanted to be closer to her than she wanted to be to you.

The following day you accompanied her to her fertility doctor, but instead of examining her, the doctor performed tests on you. It was established that you would be a suitable surrogate for her child. "A gestational carrier" was what he called you. If you had been identical twins he could have used one of your eggs, but because you were fraternal twins your sister wanted to use hers. You knew this choice of hers had to do with the fact that she felt her genes were better than yours, but you tried not to be insulted. Her superior beauty had always been a given. IVF would be used to fertilize your sister's eggs in the laboratory. If fertilization was successful, the doctor said he would transfer two or three of the resulting embryos into your uterus. He said this, and then removed his examination gloves, balled them together, and threw them in the trash.

Your husband rolled his eyes when you told him about your decision to carry your sister's child. This should have been a sign. The rolling of eyes is rarely an appropriate response for any momentous announcement, and certainly not for an act of sisterhood as profound as the one you had decided to embark on. He accused you of doing anything for your sister, and you wondered if the subtext of that comment was that you did little for him. You and your husband had previously and repeatedly discussed whether you wanted to have children together, and you were both ambivalent and swore to each other your ambivalence had nothing to do with your feelings toward each other. But of course it did.

After the second attempt at IVF with your sister and her husband's embryos, you became pregnant. They both accompanied you to the checkups, first on a monthly basis, and then on a weekly one. You read the books on pregnancy, and tried to skip over the sections on motherhood. You read in a newspaper that peppers were healthy for the fetus, and after that you couldn't stop eating them. You ate red peppers, yellow peppers, orange peppers. Every week at the grocery store you'd buy a dozen. You read poems aloud. You sang simple songs your mother had sung to you and your sister. You felt more alive than you'd felt at any time during your twenties, when you didn't have a career. You still didn't have a career, but now you had a purpose.

"Isn't there anything else you could be *passionate* about?" your husband said to you repeatedly during the pregnancy. You explained that helping your sister was the first thing you'd felt strongly about doing since diving. And you couldn't exactly make a career of diving. "You can't make a career of carrying your sister's baby either," he said.

Your sister's husband was kinder to you than your own. In the second trimester your husband had stopped trying to sleep with you altogether, and at night you wrapped yourself around the large body pillow the midwife suggested you use. You and your sister could never agree on the proper possessive pronoun for the midwife. Your sister called her "my midwife"; you called her "our midwife" or referred to her by her first name. You hoped your sister would start doing the same but she didn't.

When you suspected you were in labor, you called your sister and she came over, and when it was time, she and her husband drove you to the hospital. Your husband wasn't home; he was in Indiana on business and couldn't make it back in time. You did the math to see if he was lying and your conclusion was indecisive. Your sister's husband waited outside the delivery room while your sister knelt beside you and the midwife and the doula. Your sister soaked washcloths in cold water and placed them over your forehead. She whispered reassuring words to you. "You can do this," she said. "You can do this."

It wasn't pain so much as the most intense sensation you

had ever experienced. First the feeling of the baby trying to crawl its way down and come out into the world. Why did it feel as though it was crawling through your back? "It's trying to come out of my back," you told the midwife.

The midwife and the doula decided that to ease the pain you would be moved into the shower. They turned down the bathroom lights. The doula used her hands to massage your back while you stood in the shower. At one point, the doula asked your sister to take over massaging; she wanted to involve your sister in the delivery. Your sister's hands were not as effective.

You felt something pass through you quickly, and you screamed. The baby was coming out! You tried to catch it with your hands—it was an unwieldy shape but it fell to the shower floor and you felt an explosion of liquid on your feet. You screamed. Your sister screamed. The midwife came running back into the bathroom. "I think the baby just dropped on the shower floor," you yelled. The lights were turned on. It was explained that your water had broken.

The midwife told you you were close. You were toweled dry and moved out of the bathroom and onto a mattress that had been pulled off the bed and placed on the floor. Your sister held your hands during what no one had prepared you for— the intense burning sensation.

You tried to picture the baby. You hoped you would love it after it had tortured you so, but you immediately erased the thought. You knew you would love her.

You screamed a sound that you had never heard come from your throat. The midwife used a rag to cool off your face, to wash away your sweat or tears, or some mixture of the two. You gave one more push. The burning came again—a part of you was on fire—and then you felt the oddest sensation of your life: a person passing through your body into the world.

The midwife took the baby and counted ten toes and ten fingers. "It's a beautiful girl," she said. There was a snipping of the umbilical cord—your sister held the scissors—which was more painful than you expected. You thought the cord was not capable of sensing anything, but as she severed the cord your stomach felt as though it had been punctured by a knife. And then you were told you would have to wait for the placenta to come.

You assumed that would be easy; you had been told it would be just like menstruation—that something would slide out of you and you would be done. But it was like another child! *Was it another child?* You asked the midwife. With fertility treatments weren't multiples more likely? And besides, your sister's egg had been used and you were twins. An idea passed through your mind, an idea that had never occurred to you before but now seemed brilliant: if there were two babies, maybe you could keep one? You knew better than to voice this thought.

No, it wasn't another baby, you were told. It was the placenta. "The afterbirth," the midwife called it. And then you were pushing all over again, pushing this dreaded afterbirth out of you. "It's done," the midwife said.

It was over. It was done. And all you could hear were cries. Her cries. They were so soft. You looked at the midwife and doula, these women who had seen you at your most bare and compromised moment. You stared at your sister, not believing the intimacy you had all shared. You felt tears rolling down your cheeks and you knew they were tears of exhaustion, and tears of disappointment: you wished you had never dreamed of the possibility of giving birth to twins.

"This is the biggest gift you could ever give someone," your sister's husband said to you as he held the little baby girl. Their daughter. Not yours. Theirs.

You thanked him for thanking you and he laughed and told you that you should not be the one saying thank you.

Because the birth took place at a hospital, a nurse was required to be present in addition to the midwife and doula. The nurse wore blue scrubs and white puffy Reeboks. She carried the baby to the scale and recorded her weight, and then, using a floppy tape measure that she stretched from heel to crown of head, announced her length. The nurse in the Reeboks carried the baby back to the side of the bed where you were recuperating. She held her out for you and your sister to see. "She is *exquisite*. She looks like Cleopatra," the nurse said.

The nurse was about to hand the baby to you when your sister intercepted. "I think it's for the best if you don't hold her," she said to you.

While the film crew is adjusting the lighting you are thinking about this, all of this—the pastel flowers, your shoulder wet with your sister's tears, the body pillow, the burning sensation. You are sitting on the floor of the mosque, rocking back on your heels, with each of your palms over the opposite arm's elbow. You hear sobbing and only after a minute do you realize that it's you who's sobbing. You are the one making the wailing sounds. You open your eyes.

You notice something happening on the set around you. Or rather, you notice the absence of anything happening and your ears sense the unusual quiet. You look to your right and see the director has loosened his vise grip on his head and is staring at you. For the first time since you were introduced, he's really looking at you as a person and not as a stand-in.

"I'm sorry," you mumble. You know you've been distracted; you know you've done something wrong. No one has been this silent on set before. You wipe your face. You reposition your palms.

Now the director is talking seriously with the famous American actress. They are both staring at you. You are certain you will be fired.

You do not know what you will do for work, how you will get home. You love this job, you realize. You turn your head away. Tears don't return to your eyes, but you feel they're close. You pray in earnest—*please do not let me lose this job*—and again there is quiet all around you.

The director is staring at you.

He walks over to you. "Can I have a word?" he says.

You start to stand. You wobble with trepidation. The mosque is silent, reverential toward the punishment he is about to bestow upon you.

"No, please, don't get up," he says. You sit on the prayer rug and he sits down with you.

"That was fantastic," he says. "Stunning."

You murmur thank you, afraid he's being facetious.

He tells you he's told the famous American actress she can take a few lessons from you on how to cry.

You ask him if he really told her that.

"Of course."

Oh no, you think.

He asks you to go through the scene again, the stage directions as they've given them to you, but the emotions as you've chosen to portray them.

You do seven more takes as they adjust the lights, and then the cameras. With each new take you recall more details. You think of your sister's plea to you, her comment about the hatchet job of the abortion, the doctor's balled-up examination gloves, the insemination under bright lights, the classical music that played too loudly in your sister's husband's car as they drove you the hospital, the bright headlights of the oncoming cars, the sight of the mattress on the floor, the sensation of the baby trying to crawl through your spine, the white nightgown you planned to wear for delivery that eventually ended up in the sink of the bathroom when you were moved to the shower, your sister's incompetent massaging of your back, your waters breaking, the burning the burning the burning, your sudden and bizarre wish to be pregnant with twins, the cutting of the umbilical cord, the lemonade the doula brought you after the delivery.

When they've figured out the lights—very complicated in the mosque—and the cameras, it's the famous American actress's turn to inhabit the role of Maria. You wipe your eyes as you walk off set, and the wardrobe woman embraces you. You accept her long hug. You inhale the scent of her hair—ripe pears and cigarette smoke.

The famous American actress walks right by you and onto the set. You do not talk the rest of the day. You try not to watch as the director becomes increasingly frustrated with her performance during the scene. It occurs to you that until now, everything you have done, the actress has done after you, and has done it better. But now the director is asking her to emulate you. It's so painful you can't bear to watch, and instead look at your knees during each successive take, which becomes increasingly more difficult to endure for everyone around.

Finally, at 6 P.M. the practical secretary approaches you. "I think you need to go back to your hotel and get ready now," she says. "If you want to be on time, which I expect you do." You had forgotten about the date.

She slips you an envelope. "It's an advance on this week's payment," she says. "We want to make sure you have money in case you need it for any reason tonight. Leopoldi is a gentleman, but we don't want . . . a situation."

You don't ask her what kind of situation she might be talking about. You don't want to know. You carefully take the envelope from her hands. It's heavier than you expected and you try not to let surprise, or even delight, overtake your face.

The driver takes you back to the hotel. You're tempted to open the envelope while in the van, but you know he can see you in the rearview mirror. You have to be cautious, cool. You run your hands through your hair; you're still wearing the wig. You'll have to remember to bring it back the day after tomorrow, when you film again. He lets you off and tells you another driver will be picking you up at 7:30.

You were not aware of the extent of the puppetry of to-night's dinner: the practical secretary has instructed you to go home and change, the driver of the van is keeping you on a schedule.

You go upstairs and immediately tear open the envelope. Inside are rubber-banded stacks of Moroccan dirhams. You lie on the bed and organize the bills into various piles so you can more easily count the total. One pile for the bluish 200-dirham bills with the cargo ship and the lighthouse, an-other for the brownish hundreds with three camels and riders in the desert, a third pile for the green fifties with fruit and a bird, and a final one for the twenties with a train and an image of the King Hassan Mosque you were in earlier today. All the denominations feature the profile of a clean-shaven man you think it's safe to assume was once the king. You count 18,700 dirhams. You don't know how much this is in dollars but the number alone is intoxicating. You sniff the bills and they smell like desert heat. You stuff some of the bills in your bra, a few in each cup, and store the remainder in the hotel safe. You enter your niece's birthday as the combination to the safe.

You wash your face and reapply the makeup you bought from the plump Moroccan man in the narrow beauty shop. You slip into the green silk dress. You don't recognize the de-signer's name but you know it must be expensive. The silk is wrinkled, the belt on the side.

You wear your flat sandals. You have no purse, so you slip your hotel key card beneath the front clasp of your bra. You look in the mirror and worry he'll be disappointed. You put on the wig.

In the lobby the concierge points to a driver, a different one, without stepping out from behind his desk. The driver nods hello to you rather than shaking your hand, and escorts you outside. Town cars are common at the Regency, but not at the Grand Hotel, and you notice more than one guest staring as the driver opens the door to the backseat for you.

He doesn't talk to you during the short duration of the drive. The restaurant is on one of the piers you saw on the police chief's large map of the city. It's like most piers at night—there's a strange mix of efficiency and menace, as though someone's being deposited in the ocean, but will be first wrapped carefully in white sheets.

The driver opens the door for you and you step out into the evening air, which smells of salt but also inexplicably like roses. Casablanca is on the brink of summer and you briefly recall an Emily Dickinson poem you read in high school about the brevity of spring, before you realize you don't remember it at all. Only that it was about the brevity of spring. The driver tells you that it's his understanding that he will not be waiting because "Monsieur" will be driving you home.

He waits for a tip. You discreetly remove a couple bills from the cup of your bra. You have no idea what the exchange rate is. You give him ten dirhams and you can tell by his reaction it's not enough so you add ten more.

As soon as you exit the town car you feel less optimistic

despite the spring air. Once the driver leaves, you will be alone with the Russian businessman who has been on several dates with the famous American actress. He will be unhappy to see you. You have no ride home.

You make sure your dress is falling appropriately across your body—aside from not having the money, this is why you don't buy designer dresses: they rarely drape correctly.

You climb the stairs of the restaurant, the walls covered with fishnets and ships' wheels. At the top, near a topless mermaid that once helmed a ship that most likely sank, you tell the maître d' that someone is expecting you.

You see your date standing in the corner of the room. He has a prime table with a view. He's in his late forties, wearing a suit and tie. He's tall and wide and not as unattractive as you expected, given that the famous American actress is passing him on to you. You know it's him because he stands with his arms outstretched and with an expression that seems about to say, *Darling!* in Russian except that he doesn't. He places his arms back at his sides and gives you a quizzical look.

You walk up and greet him. You shake his hand and tell him your name is Reeves.

"So she's not coming?" he says. His accent is less Russian and more global than you expected.

You tell him that filming is running late.

"Right," he says. "And I'm supposed to believe you?"

You have no answer for this; you didn't expect him to be so skeptical. You see the profound disappointment—even anger—on his face, and reassure him she'll very likely be stopping by later. She said no such thing to you.

He extends his hand toward your chair. It's turned toward the window and this is your first clue that he cares about the famous American actress. If he simply wanted to show her off, he would have seated her so she faced out at the room. But she—and now you—are expected to face the window, out of which you can see a darkening sky but little of the ocean, and nothing of the pier on which the restaurant is situated.

You offer him a brief smile. His nose looks like it was broken, and he has a scar on his right cheek. His hair is gray but still thick. He offers no smile in return; he simply stares at you like you're a practical item in a store that he's deliberating whether he wants to buy.

The waiter approaches. He's an older Moroccan man with tired eyes, as though he's been working at this restaurant for too many years and has seen too many tourists, too many poorly matched couples. He asks if you'd like drinks. You expect the businessman to tell the waiter that you won't be staying, that there's been a mistake.

"Gin and tonic?" he says to you.

You nod. It's what the famous American actress drinks. You wonder if she started drinking them with him, or if he's ordering them because he knows she likes them and he's thinking of her.

"So who are you, exactly?" he says. "What do you do for her?"

You tell him you're her stand-in on set. Just for this film, you explain.

"And now you're standing in for her date with me," he says matter-of-factly.

You explain again that she has to work late. It sounds less and less convincing. You scratch your head, and feel the wig. You'd almost forgotten you were wearing it. You regret putting it on. You exhale so that the bangs will fly up and out of your eyes.

"What's your name?" he asks.

For a flicker of a moment you have difficulty placing your current identity; the wig threw you off. You tell him again your name is Reeves.

"Reeves, I'm Leopoldi. But you probably know that."

He sips his gin and tonic, and with wet lips he says, "Let's not pretend. We both know she's not coming. She thinks I'm going to be upset because she's been in the tabloids lately with that boy who I'm sure is gay. Am I jealous?"

You think it's a rhetorical question but it's not. He wants you to answer.

No, you tell him. You don't think he's jealous.

"Reeves! What world do you come from?" he says. "Of course I'm jealous. But I wasn't going to yell at her about it. She'll find out soon enough he's gay and come back to me. Don't you think he's gay?"

You know this is not a good time to add your opinion that the boyfriend is not gay.

"Well, let's make it a nice meal, Reeves. Are you in agreement?"

You clink glasses.

"To a nice meal," he says.

The gin and tonic has an immediate effect on him. You can see him relaxing and he loosens his tie. His tie is expensive-looking and, like all expensive ties, has a stupid pattern—this one has little frogs. You wish he would take it off.

He sees you staring at the tie.

"Isn't this the ugliest tie you've seen in your life?" he says.

You can't help it: you let out a laugh.

"You were thinking that, weren't you? You were wondering why a handsome man like me would wear a tie like this. It is a tie for idiots."

You weren't thinking that he was handsome, but you don't correct him on this point.

"Yes," you say. "As a matter of fact, that's exactly what I was thinking."

"She sent it to me from Japan. From that movie she was doing there. The one with the montage of her eating fifty different bowls of rice."

You know which film he's talking about. You chose not to see it.

"My guess is it wasn't her who picked it out but the secretary," you venture. "She has this very practical secretary who handles her life. She's maybe twenty years older and smiling for her is a considerable challenge."

"Are you trying to make me feel better?" Leopoldi says. "Is that supposed to make me feel better? That she had her secretary pick out a romantic present for me?" He seems incensed and his face pinkens as though the tie is choking him.

You apologize. You are thinking that you should leave before the drinks are finished; you have made a colossal error.

"Reeves! I'm just messing with you. Of course that makes me feel better. I was going around thinking that she had the worst taste in the world picking out this tie with these toads on it. I mean, who would pick out such a thing?"

His laugh is uproarious. He laughs like a larger man than he is. Maybe it's the money, you think. Maybe when you have that much money in the bank you can laugh uproariously like a very large man at things that aren't that funny.

Soon you've both had two gin and tonics. You need the food to come to absorb what you have had to drink. You turn slightly, your eyes searching for the waiter. The restaurant is starting to fill up with wealthy Moroccans and tourists. People sit at tables in strange configurations of four or seven or three, like they're stars in constellations that will never be named. A man with pale skin and hair that used to be strawberry blond but has faded to a strange yellow gray, like a polluted sunset, is sitting by himself, drinking a beer and eating scallops. He's in his forties. His table faces your table, and it's a little disconcerting. You try not to look in his direction. The gin and tonics are getting into your head. You need the food to come.

When it arrives you dig into the black bass. The salad is sad-looking with leaky tomatoes and lettuce so pale it's white. But the bass is fresh.

"I like a woman with an appetite," Leopoldi says to you.

You smile with your mouth full.

You realize the conversation is bound to turn more personal. You don't want him to ask you about yourself. You will need to ask him about him, about his business; you will need to act riveted by his responses.

"What do you do?" you ask. "It must be wonderful."

"Which business are you talking about?" he says, again laughing and finding this overly entertaining. "I own many companies."

You ask him what his favorite is.

"My favorite company," he says. "That's like asking a man who his favorite child is."

You ask if he has children.

"Not a good topic right now," he tells you. "There's some paternity testing going on."

He seems upset with you. He focuses on his food. You want to remind him that he's the one who brought up children.

But then a bottle of wine arrives and his mood brightens. The waiter pours you each a glass of Chardonnay.

"You were asking about my favorite business," he says. "It's a cosmetic laser. A better one than what's out there right now. For scars, acne," he explains. He's looking at your face. He leans over and softly takes your chin in his large hand, and tilts your head to the side. With the fingers of his left hand he brushes the bangs of the wig out of your face so that he can see you more clearly.

It's an intimate gesture—one that takes you by surprise. He studies your face so intently that for a moment you think you might cry. You don't think your husband ever examined your features so closely, that he ever moved your hair out of your face. This was in large part why you married him. You liked the fact that he never stole glances at you, that he turned off the lights before you kissed. You thought that with him you could be invisible, until you realized that wasn't at all what you wanted.

"May I ask what happened to your skin?" Leopoldi says. Tiny tears are forming in the corner of your eyes, but he doesn't wish to embarrass you by asking about them. Instead he says: "Despite your makeup I can see . . ."

"Teenage acne," you explain.

He nods, and lets go of your chin gently. You would not have expected him to be so careful with his touch.

"And you," you say, emboldened by his question, by his caress. "May I ask about your scar?"

He puts down his fork and knife. This is going to be a story. "I wasn't always so wealthy," he tells you. "I grew up poor in a little town between Moscow and St. Petersburg. On a farm. I was helping my father with the fence one day, a new barbed-wire fence to keep the sheep from getting away. My brother was driving a tractor and I was attaching the wire to the fence, when it sprung out of my hand and slashed across my face."

You have this in common——the marks of the past on your skin. You both look out the window, as though wanting to focus on the beauty of the outside world. But the sun has set now and you see only your own reflections.

"I have a plan!" he says, both boisterously and boastfully, turning back from the window to you. "I made a reservation at Rick's Café for a nightcap," he says. "Of course that's when I thought she was coming, and not you, but it's a great place. Have you been?"

You ask if he means the same Rick's Café from *Casablanca*.

"Not the same one, that was just a stage set in, I believe, Culver City," he says.

You are surprised he knows about Culver City.

"But," he continues, "the woman who owns this one is American and she fixed it up so it looks like the one in the movie. There's even a piano player."

It does sound appealing. And you don't have much choice but to go. You promised the famous American actress you'd make sure he had a good evening. And you have no other ride back to the hotel.

A driver in a town car waits for the two of you in the parking lot. The driver opens the door for you on one side, and then goes around to the other side to open it for Leopoldi. You thank Leopoldi for dinner and he seems touched that you thanked him.

In the distance you can hear the music from Jazzablanca. "I called ahead and asked for a special table," he says. "I said we needed discretion because of who she was."

This of course means that when you arrive at Rick's Café Americain—which has the exact neon sign outside that you remember from the film—there's no discretion at all. The hostess is overly polite to you as she walks you, slowly, through the main dining area, which is spanned by arches. The tablecloths and cushions are white, the walls and arches are white. The restaurant is crowded with diners speaking English, Spanish, and French, and there is indeed a piano player rushing through "As Time Goes By." A few tourists smoke cigars at the bar; you can tell by the way they're holding them that they don't usually smoke cigars, but they want to act like they're in another time period. You see a few heads turn as you pass by. You're wearing the wig so your hair is like hers; you're wearing her dress. You know what they are all thinking: *In real life she's not as beautiful.*

You are seated upstairs in a private area shrouded by large palm leaves. Your back is to the other diners and drinkers. Leopoldi orders you a drink called "the Ingrid" and orders himself a vodka.

"I was just drinking gin and tonics before because that's what she likes to drink," he says. Because your head is clouded with alcohol, it takes you a minute to remember that by *she* he means the famous American actress, and not your sister. "Real Russians, we drink our vodka. Vodka is our water." The more he drinks, the more he sounds like the Russian farm boy he was.

You drink the Ingrid through a straw. You do not want him to ask you about yourself. You know that to be a good liar you have to remember your lies, and you're in a state of drunkenness in which you're having trouble remembering much at all.

When you finish your drink you feel a little lopsided in your chair, like you're slumping, so you adjust yourself and . . . boom. You are on the floor. Leopoldi is squeezing around the table to help you up but you also sense something bright out of the corner of your eye. It's the white lightning of flash. A tourist is taking a photo of you, a photo showing how drunk you are that you fell to the ground. "Stop," you say, and hold up your hand in the direction of the flash attack. It won't stop. This tourist will not stop taking photos.

Leopoldi helps you up, and escorts you to the car. You roll down the window—*see, I'm not drunk, I'm in control*—and the car speeds and stops and speeds as you zoom your way to the

Grand Hotel. You inhale deeply, taking in the dirty night air. You decide you must watch *Casablanca* again, you must buy souvenirs for your mother who has never been to Morocco and who always loves to collect clothing and shoes from far-away lands, you must be in constant touch with your niece throughout her entire life.

Leopoldi helps you up to your room, and asks for your key. You don't have it, you say. He suggests you both go down to the lobby. He says he would do it but they wouldn't believe him without you or your ID so you should both go to the lobby and request another copy of your room key. You know very little right now, but know this will be a disaster. You have no ID and you are registered under the previous stand-in's name. Miraculously, under pressure, you remember your key is secured under the front clasp of your bra. You hand the now-warm key card to Leopoldi and he lets you into the room.

He stands on the threshold.

"It was a nice evening," he says. "I'm sorry I overserved you."

You intend to thank him for being a gentleman, for standing on the other side of the threshold. You move your mouth—why is it so difficult to move your mouth?—and the door closes on him, loudly. The bed seems miles away. You drop onto your knees and use the foot of the mattress as a pillow for your tired and heavy head.

In the early morning the phone rings. Your brain feels like it's just been broken into seven continents. You pick up the phone because you're still half asleep; if you were awake you'd ignore its obscenely loud shrieks.

The practical secretary is on the phone. She does not say good morning; she instructs you to be in the Regency's tenth-floor lounge in half an hour. You shower the scent of alcohol off your skin. You plan to get to the lounge quickly so you can order a strong coffee to ease your headache.

You rush through the Regency lobby so you won't be spotted by the manager. You arrive at the lounge early, but the practical secretary and the famous American actress are already there, waiting. There's no sign of the waiter you usually see. You have the distinct impression that he's been dismissed so this meeting could be private.

"Good morning," you say, but it comes out sounding like a question.

The famous American actress looks livid. She speaks first. "I told you to go out with him. I didn't say you should make him fall for you."

You've never seen her like this. There's a fury inside her that is terrifying. You understand how she's made it this far in her career. She's a missile that's been launched and can't be halted.

"I'm sorry," you say. "I don't think that's true."

The actress's eyes narrow on you. "My psycho radar is usually much better. Are you looking for a wealthy husband?"

You have no idea what's happening. There's a narrative here that you're not privy to.

"I really don't know what you're talking about," you say. "You asked me to go. I went. I tried to be nice. We got along fine. He was wearing the tie you bought him. We talked about you most of the night."

"Really?" she says. "Because the text I got from him said that he was happy I didn't show up. That he had more fun with *you*."

"Listen," you say. "I have no interest in him. I don't have his phone number. He doesn't have mine. I did what you asked."

There is no coffee. There is no waiter to bring coffee.

"Did you?" she says. Her skin seems to barely contain a raging bonfire inside.

You try to make eye contact with the bodyguards who are seated at the other side of the room; you may need their help if she physically attacks you. The one with the reddish hair, the one you talked with about radical speciation and what to feed a turtle, sees you trying to make eye contact with him. He turns his head the other way.

The practical secretary jumps in. "We have much more serious matters to discuss," she says. "Do you realize you were photographed?"

"You got wasted!" the famous American actress says. "And why the fuck were you wearing the wig?"

"Some tourist took a slew of photos of you falling down on the floor drunk," the practical secretary says. "You were a mess. The photos are terrible."

You don't know what to say. "Okay. I don't know why that's a problem. Why would anyone care that a stand-in drank too much?"

The famous American actress almost jumps out of her seat. "It's a fucking problem because they think it's me, you stupid bitch! Because you were wearing the wig! Who told you to wear the fucking wig? Everyone thought you were me."

"There's no way," you say. "We don't look—"

"You were wearing the wig! You were wearing my dress! I've been photographed in that dress. It's my designer! You were with a man people know I dated. It was supposed to be *discreet*. I assumed you would stay sober. Instead you got drunk, fell off a chair, and rolled around like a pig. What the fuck is wrong with you?"

"Please," the practical secretary says, looking imploringly at the famous American actress. "We have to clean this up now. We have real, pressing questions here." The practical secretary turns back to you. "This is what's going on. The tourist has retained one of these bottom-feeding lawyer intermediaries. He's contacted us saying if we don't pay a certain sum they'll sell the photos to the tabloids. We're trying to formulate a plan here but I don't know if we have any good options."

"You know how much your little stunt is going to cost?" the famous American actress asks. "One hundred thousand dollars—minimum. That's if they don't raise the price sometime today."

There's a small part of you that's amused that any photo of you could ever be worth that much.

"Are you smirking?" the practical secretary asks. Your brief amusement must have showed itself on your face. "Do you think this is funny?"

You hear the exasperation in her voice. She's furious with you as well. You should be seeking the bodyguards' attention so they can protect you from the practical secretary, not the famous American actress. You have made a grave error, and you will be punished.

"No, I don't think it's funny at all," you say honestly to the practical secretary. Her face is so twisted now that you can't look at her. You turn to the famous American actress. "Do you care that much about not looking drunk?" you say. A few nights ago she was throwing back gin and tonics while wearing pajamas patterned with pastel hippos. She didn't seem to care then.

"I care that much about not looking like I'm cheating on my boyfriend," the famous American actress says. "That's the reason I sent you out with Leopoldi in the first place! So no one could say I was cheating on my boyfriend!"

"I'm sure we can explain everything," you say.

"Why don't you explain why you're fucking trying to ruin my life?" she screams. She stares at you as though she actually wants an answer.

"I only did what you asked," you say.

"Fuck you, Reeves," she says. "Or whatever the fuck your name is. What is your name? Where's your passport?"

She stares at you, but addresses the practical secretary: "Ask to see her passport." She storms out of the lounge. The bodyguards follow her.

"I apologize for her behavior," the practical secretary says unapologetically.

"I take it for granted that I'm fired," you say.

"No," the practical secretary says. "We can't fire you. The insurers are already concerned about her temper. It's been a problem in the past."

"But you saw the way she is with me. And my passport—"

"No, stop," the practical secretary says, and holds her hand up. "Whatever you're going to tell me, I don't want to know." She places a palm over each ear like she's one of the three monkeys. "I have enough on my plate right now, thanks to you," she says. "Tomorrow's a big day of shooting. You've already potentially cost us a hundred thousand. If you're not there you cost the production much more."

You don't know what to say.

"So we'll see you tomorrow," she says.

She stands up and leaves.

You are alone in the tenth-floor lounge.

The bartender enters the room, confirming your earlier suspicion that he was dismissed during the meeting.

"Can I please have a coffee?" you ask him.

"Are you a guest at the hotel?" he asks. Even he knows you have been shunned.

"Forget it," you say, and stand up and leave.

You return to your room at the Grand and look out the window. The band shell that used to be outside in the plaza is gone—Jazzablanca must be over. The plaza appears more somber now, the pedestrians more serious as they walk with long strides and purpose.

Today is your day off work, and it feels interminable. There are too many directions the day could take. The photo could be sold to the tabloids. That would be disastrous for the famous American actress, and for you. But what concerns you most at this moment is the fact that the actress knows you are not Reeves Conway. She knows that you have no ID of your own, that you're in possession of a passport that doesn't belong to you. You should not have told her that your passport was stolen, that the police gave you the belongings of someone named Sabine Alyse. You have little faith that she will keep this information to herself. Even if the practical secretary covers her ears when the famous American actress tries to tell her about it—and surely she will try—there is someone who will want to listen to the famous American actress tell them that you've been staying under a fake name, that you are in possession of a passport that doesn't belong to you. Again, you picture Sabine Alyse's face. You haven't looked at her passport photo since the day it was handed to you by the police; when you picture her now, she's pale, unconscious.

You don't know why you have held on to Sabine Alyse's passport, credit cards, journal, and backpack. You should have disposed of them the day you were offered the job as the stand-in. You have been on a film set in the home of a wealthy Moroccan, in the tenth-floor lounge drinking gin and tonics with a famous American actress, at a Patti Smith concert, in a mosque, at dinner with a Russian businessman, and all the while you've been in possession of the belongings of a young woman who is most likely dead. If she's not dead, she's in trouble. You have to make an effort not to think about the single line you read in her journal: *I tried to tell them it wasn't dangerous.*

A sudden urgency expands within you. You know you

need to get rid of the backpack, the diary, the wallet, the passport. All the famous American actress has to do is make one phone call and your hotel room will be searched, and you will be arrested for theft. Or more. You will be questioned. You will be brought to the American embassy and Susan Sontag will connect the dots. You do not trust the famous American actress, you don't trust anyone. You know the police will be of no help.

You could cut the passport, and credit cards and the pages of the diary into pieces, and throw everything into the wastepaper basket in the bathroom. Still, everything could be traced back to your room, to your wastepaper basket, to you. And there would remain the problem of what to do with the backpack and wallet.

You can't return the items to the police. That's out of the question. If she is alive she's reported all her possessions stolen. You have to be rid of them—of everything related to Sabine Alyse.

You enter your niece's date of birth as the code to unlock the safe, and remove the passport and diary and wallet. You dump out all the clothes from your suitcase. Her backpack is at the bottom. You place the diary inside the main pocket of the backpack. You put the passport and wallet in the external pocket and don't zip it closed all the way. The royal-blue corner of the passport is visible. The wallet is just in front of it. Your plan is to go to the market in the old medina, walk around, and wait for the inevitable theft.

You remove fifty dirhams from the safe—you don't want to carry too much—and place them in your bra.

You take a taxi to the market. You place the backpack over one shoulder and walk past the merchants selling dark brown leather backpacks. "Backpack, backpack," they say to you. You want to tell them you already have one that you're trying to get rid of. Instead you keep your eyes ahead of you and continue walking.

It's crowded in the marketplace and it smells like cats, though none are visible. You pass spice stands in a row, displaying spices of golden yellow, burnt orange, and poppy red in shallow, circular woven baskets. The displays are exactly what you expected of a spice shop here, and the shops' popularity with tourists leads you to suspect the shopkeepers have studied pictures in the guidebooks to Morocco. They're giving the tourists precisely what they pictured Morocco would look like. You keep moving.

"*Pardonnez-moi,*" you say as you delve deeper into the crowds. You pass a young man selling birdcages without the birds. You stand before him, and place the backpack by your feet. You know it's careless; you worry that your carelessness will not be appreciated and you'll have to be more obvious, more irresponsible. You open the birdcages and close them, making sure the doors close properly. As though this matters.

Finally your curiosity has to be satisfied. You look down. The backpack is gone. You turn in a circle. No one suspicious is around you. You look behind you: a complicated braid of pedestrians.

You are free of Sabine Alyse. You are free from any implications about her fate.

You take a right and another right until you exit the marketplace. You hail a taxi and return to your hotel room at the Grand. No messages have been slipped under your door, and the light on the hotel phone isn't blinking. You start to imagine that the practical secretary exaggerated the gravity of the situation. Why has no one been in touch? You watch the phone for twenty minutes. You pick it up to make sure it's working.

At 7 P.M. the sides for the following morning are slipped beneath your door. A note scrawled on the envelope says: *Wardrobe says you didn't return the wig. Please remember it tomorrow.* You don't know whose handwriting it is.

You open the envelope. Pickup in the morning will be at 8 A.M. and filming will take place at the American embassy. Impossible! You think of Susan Sontag. Will she be there? Your worries begin all over again. You'll be wearing the wig, so there's a chance she won't recognize you, but what will you do if she does?

You try to watch a movie on TV but soon discover it's about a woman who gets arrested. You turn it off. You fall asleep with great difficulty, wake repeatedly, and rise early.

There's still no word from the practical secretary. You can only assume this is good news. You get dressed and put on the wig so you don't forget it. You're afraid of Susan Sontag and need to make sure you arrive at the embassy in some sort of disguise. You remove your money from the safe, divide it into two, and place a stack in each cup of your bra. You have half an hour before the producers will be meeting you in the van. You go to the hotel's business center so you can get online and confirm that the photo hasn't gotten out.

You type in the famous American actress's name and search for any news. The computer shows that two minutes before, the photo of you at Rick's Café was posted by a British tabloid. The headline is HERE'S LOOKING AT YOU, KID. You can only assume that the tabloid offered so much money that the bottom-feeding lawyer didn't come back to the practical secretary. You assume she will be as surprised as anyone to find the photo posted. You know something went horribly wrong.

You study the photo. In it, you are taken aback by how much you look like the famous American actress. Your hand is outstretched, trying to block the photographer, but this only makes it more convincing that it's a photo of an actress accustomed to fending off paparazzi. Leopoldi is standing behind you, trying to help you up. It's clearly him.

You refresh the computer. Before your eyes the number of news stories has multiplied—the photo's been linked to by thirteen sites. When it's been picked up by twenty-one sites, you turn the computer screen off, as though that will prevent the photo from spreading further.

You are dizzy, your stomach a volcanic pit, as you sit on the bench outside the hotel, waiting for the van. You know what scandal the producers will be talking about today; you know what everyone will be talking about. You wonder if the producers will know it wasn't the famous American actress in the photo.

If the famous American actress was about to tear into you yesterday, you can only imagine what she'll do today, now that the photo has been published, linked to, commented upon. You're afraid she'll publicly accuse you of not being who you claim you are. And she'll be doing this on set at the American embassy. It would be insane for you to put yourself at that kind of risk of exposure. You cannot continue working on the film. You cannot remain anywhere where the famous American actress or the practical secretary could find you.

While you've been sitting on the bench outside the hotel, tourists have been boarding a large white bus. You recognize it as the same large white bus that was outside the hotel on your first day of work as a stand-in, when you mistakenly thought the bus was your transportation to set. You see the same tour guide with his silver clipboard at the stairs to the bus. Where did he say the tour went?

You stand and walk as casually as you can toward the bus. "Meknes?" he says. You nod, and he tells you he will be collecting the fare on the bus. You board.

Three dozen men and women are already seated on the plush seats. Most of them are couples in their sixties. The women wear long pants and open-toed shoes; their husbands look like they've shrunk in recent years, their bodies condensed with gravity and age. Even their collared polo shirts look a size too big.

You quickly find a seat in the middle. The tour guide is coming down the aisle and collecting money and marking numbers down on his clipboard. You try to see how many dirhams everyone else is giving him so you can remove the appropriate amount from your bra. As he approaches you, you hand him what you have discerned is the correct payment, and then turn to look out the window. You see the young American producer and the Indian producer get into the van. Their eyes are searching the front of the hotel; they're most likely looking for you.

You instinctively take off the wig and move to the other side of the bus and sit by the opposite window. Two women board the bus. One of them looks vaguely familiar. She speaks English with an American accent and she has dark hair with thick, blond highlights. You glance at her shoes, fearing you'll see puffy white Reeboks. Instead, she's wearing blue Converses, with zippers on the side. And she's not wearing glasses or a Florida State University sweatshirt, nor is she traveling in a large group of women on a college reunion tour. You tell yourself to relax: you're being paranoid. What are the odds that she's on this bus? You arrived in Casablanca on the same flight over a week ago. Or maybe you didn't—you are beginning to believe you imagined the nurse's presence on the plane. You have not been yourself lately.

The tour guide comes up the aisle from behind and stops by your row. Apparently you didn't pay him enough money because he's asking for more. You remove the bills from the cup of your bra and hand them to the guide. He looks away, as though embarrassed about what he's seen. You stare straight ahead: you're afraid that if you look out the window of the bus you'll see the pale practical secretary's face searching for yours.

You contemplate being free of the actress and the practical secretary. This is of foremost importance. All you need to do now is get to Meknes, and you'll figure out your plan from there. You take inventory of what you've left in your room—a suitcase full of clothes you don't like. A toothbrush. The only thing you'll regret leaving behind is the foundation you bought from the man in the Casablanca beauty shop. You tell yourself you can stop by there again when you're back in Casablanca, but you already know you'll never come back. You wait for the bus to start. You need it to leave. Until it's departed you can still be found.

Finally: the hum of the loud engine. The bus begins to slowly roll out of the Grand Hotel's parking lot. Once it's made its way onto the main street, and passes by a gas station that says LIBYA OIL, you lean your head against the window, close your eyes, and fall asleep.

When you wake Casablanca is far behind you. You pass olive groves, small farms. A few wiry dogs run alongside the bus, barking, until they seem satisfied the bus is leaving their territory and cease their chase. It's brighter out than it's been since you arrived in Morocco. The sun stretches out its rays long and wide, as though it's been trapped in tight quarters and is finally free to expand.

For the first time since you arrived in Morocco, you wish you had a camera to document the terrain. You want to remember all of this—the bright sunlight, the smattering of red flowers, the small houses, built of dark wood.

You think of the expensive Pentax camera you purchased toward the end of the pregnancy, to document your belly, to document the birth. You had photos on that camera of you and the baby, photos you never backed up because you didn't have time to read the instructions before your trip. Now you have no photos of you and baby Reeves together. You noticed that your sister and her husband didn't take any of the two of you. At the time, you told yourself it was an oversight. So you took a series of photos of you holding the baby. You held her cradled in one arm and stretched out the other arm and kept your finger on the camera's button until she started to cry from the flash.

In an hour the bus approaches the small city of Meknes. You see the long ocher wall of an old city, a green minaret in the distance. The tour guide, who has short black hair and a compact body, looks around thirty. He stands with a microphone, and after telling you that he has a degree in history, he begins a lecture about the history of Meknes: how it used to be the capital of Morocco, how the sultan Moulay Ismaïl, who reigned in the seventeenth century, was known as the Sun King of Morocco. He built everything on a massive scale, surrounding the city with walls and bastions and protecting it with monumental gateways. You stop listening and stare out the window. Though the walls are high, the city looks small and manageable next to the chaotic expanse of Casablanca.

The bus stops in a large parking lot, next to other tour buses. You descend from the bus and your group of three dozen forms a bloblike shape in the dusty lot. A half-dozen men in caftans, some with vertical black stripes and others a solid oatmeal color, hold small, squat stools and offer to polish shoes. The tour guide barks at them, driving them away. Then he makes an announcement that you will start off touring the Sun King of Morocco's former palace and stables be-

fore walking through the souks. He warns you that the streets
are mazelike and confusing and emphasizes the need to stick
close together. He tells you he will be carrying a large green
umbrella so you can follow it if you get lost. As he announces
this, he opens the umbrella and holds it up so you can see what
a large green umbrella looks like.

While you are listening to the tour guide who once studied
history, and seems intent on telling you everything he once
learned, three white vans pull up. Fourteen or so men and a
few women emerge from the vans. Many of them are wearing vests, some are carrying tape recorders and cameras. The
average age of the group is twenty years younger than your
tour group. If you're not mistaken it's a press pool—the journalists are surrounding a man who appears to be some kind of
dignitary. They're taking photos, writing down what he says.

The shoeshine men approach them, and are again promptly
dismissed.

"What's going on there?" one of the shrinking husbands
in your group asks the tour guide. The guide looks over at the
press pool.

"I think it's the ambassador from Nigeria," he says. "I read
in the paper that he would be in town with his entourage. We
will let them go first. Not that we have a choice. They always
get to go wherever they want. I've heard they don't even need
passports since they fly on private planes." The tour guide
looks as though he would spit if it didn't make him look un-
dignified.

You are envious of how quickly the press pool seems to
move. They don't need to stand outside the palace being lec-

tured about how they will be following an umbrella. The press pool moves together with energy and zest. They make their way into the palace quickly, and are out of sight.

Meanwhile you are still standing in a dusty parking lot with a group of elderly Americans being lectured about the Sun King of Morocco. The tour guide tells you the king had six hundred wives from all over the world. Half of your tour group makes some sort of exclamation. "Don't get any ideas, honey," one of the women says to her shrinking husband. Everyone in the group laughs.

"He also had countless children," the tour guide continues. How many children might he have had with six hundred wives? You do the math. You don't think you've ever heard the word "countless" used so correctly. You wonder how often the king would visit each wife. Once a year? Did he have a favorite? He must have had a favorite he returned to over and over again. You imagine how the other wives felt toward her.

You quickly learn that this must be a very cheap tour. Your guide doesn't lead you into the palace's rooms, but instead escorts you to the stables, which are now a series of drab walls with arches. "Arab historians claimed that the royal stables could hold a cavalry of twelve hundred horses," the guide informs you. The walls are crumbling, the architecture plain and, aside from its immensity, unremarkable. Everyone in your group takes photos, hundreds of photos.

You are already tired of the group, of its glacial pace. It gets worse when you exit the stables and move into the souks.

The narrow, twisting alleyways of Meknes cannot accommodate a tour group of this size. You follow the group through multiple arches. Shoes for sale dangle like mistletoe. You look up and are afraid of a sole slapping your face, so you immediately bring your head down again. You pass a small narrow shop where a man dressed in white weaves an ivory tablecloth with incredible speed. His hands are moving so quickly you can barely make out his fingers. The man's young son stands several feet in front of him, his short young arms extended, each hand holding an enormous spool of thread for his father.

As the group squeezes through the narrow alleyways you're ashamed to be part of a tour. You're ashamed of the guide, who carries an opened umbrella above his head though there's no chance of rain and speaks loudly, too loudly. You try to tune in to other sounds. Around you chickens squawk though you can't see them and tourists barter with shop-keepers. You inhale the scents of meals being cooked in the apartments above. You smell saffron, garlic, lamb. You are suddenly ravenous. It's approaching lunchtime.

Several members of your group want to stop in a shoe store. "There's a better one ahead," the tour guide says. "We'll be there in a few minutes." You suspect that the tour guide has an agreement with some of the shopkeepers, that he gets compensation for bringing his group to some vendors rather than others.

You pass silversmiths hammering away at small black sculptures of gazelles. You come face-to-face with the head of a stag for sale. You pass dozens of rug shops, the rugs displayed on walls like tapestries. They smell of sour heat, like clothes that have just been removed from a dryer after remaining wet for too long. You pass a fruit stand with oranges stacked in a triangle, apples in a miniature hill.

As you make your way through the narrow maze, following the ridiculous umbrella, your group forces all other humans to the walls. There are other tourists, yes—some of them dressed in caftans—but also local men, women, and children trying to get on with their day, trying to return to their homes that sit behind the short doors that line the streets. Men carrying crates and stools, and women weighed down by heavy plastic bags filled with groceries and fabric, turn sideways to squeeze past your group. You see the frustration and annoyance on their faces, and you understand. You and your group are an obstacle. You're tempted to run away from the group but that would serve no purpose: the marketplace is so labyrinthine and tight that you're afraid you'll become lost; you're afraid that as a single traveler alone you'll be more conspicuous. As it is now, the locals' hostility can be directed toward a tour group and not toward you. You stick close to the group as you navigate the cobblestoned streets. Every few minutes, a member of your group trips.

The guide leads you into a shoe shop and greets the owner warmly by name, confirming your suspicion that he has an agreement with this one. "These shoes are called babouche," the tour guide says. "They are for men and women. My friend here makes beautiful ones." The shoes are pointed leather slippers. They come in turquoise, lime green, and the bright colors of berries. The heel of one slipper is tucked into the other, and they're displayed on the wall in an organized pattern. Not unlike decorative tiles, you think. No space of the wall is left uncovered. The small shop smells of leather, and now that it's been taken over by your group, the leather scent has been combined with the stench of body odor. You buy a pair of orange slippers for your mother.

You exit the shop and wait on the street outside. Above you are signs instructing you to VISIT HERE. Everyone wants shoppers to visit their store but they give no description of what their store sells. You don't want to deviate from the group but you can tell they're going to take a while. You buy a yellow square of candy with almonds inside, and eat it right away. You buy a bright blue and white caftan for your mother from a man wearing an argyle sweater vest over a white cotton polo shirt. He tells you that the caftans for women are called djellabas, and shows you that the one you bought has a blue hood. From this same man you buy a small basket to use as a purse for your purchases—the slippers and djellaba. He seems relieved that you don't try to barter with him.

Clothes hang around you and float above you like ghosts. Men's pants, women's djellabas, soccer shirts for boys that say MESSI. Almost immediately after purchasing your djellaba you see a green one that your mother would like more, and regret purchasing the one in your basket.

It takes a good twenty-five minutes for your group to exit the shoe store. The guide holds up his umbrella and instructs everyone to follow him for lunch. He leads you back to the bus.

At first you don't understand why you didn't eat in the souks, but once you've all boarded the bus, the tour guide explains. "We're going to drive five minutes to a very good restaurant. My friend owns this restaurant and he will give you a good deal." Of course you are going to his friend's restaurant. You are confident that the tour guide is getting a good deal as well.

The tour guide counts heads and then counts again. Then he counts a third time. He makes his way down the aisle of the bus, pointing his index finger at each passenger's face as he counts everyone on one side of the bus. Then he repeats the process on the other side of the bus, pointing to each person and mumbling numbers to himself. When he walks up to the front again you notice he walks faster. He says something to the bus driver. Then he takes out the microphone and makes an announcement: "We are still waiting for someone to return to the bus, so we will stay here for a few more minutes before moving on."

You sit and look out the window, waiting to see if the missing person is approaching. You don't know if the person is male or female, so you just stare. You see a car with a young Italian-looking couple pull into the parking lot. They park and then get out of the car. They look around for signs to see if they're allowed to park where they are.

A middle-aged Moroccan man in a *thobe* has been watching them. He approaches the couple and you assume he's saying they must pay him for parking in the spot they have chosen. The Italian man reaches down into the lower thigh pockets of his cargo pants and extracts a few coins. You doubt that the man who charged them the fee has anything to do with the parking lot.

The tour guide speaks with the bus driver again. Then he exits the bus and stands by the door, as though the stray passenger is like a dog that will come running if his owner is in sight. You half expect the tour guide to whistle.

Fifteen minutes have passed. Your fellow passengers are getting restless the way people do in vehicles that aren't moving. You're all sitting facing forward, but not going anywhere. A few of the others stand up to stretch or to retrieve something from a purse or bag that's stored above their seats. Some start passing around items they purchased in the souks, the way soon-to-be brides pass around presents at a shower.

Outside, the tour guide makes a call on his cell phone. You imagine it's to his supervisor or someone at the tour bus headquarters. When he boards the bus again he looks like he's trying to mimic the expression of someone who's in control. His head is lifted, his jaw firm.

He makes an announcement. He is going to break everyone up into groups of two or three and ask everyone to return to the market to find the missing passenger and help lead them back. He emphasizes how important it is that you stick together in teams so that another one of you doesn't go missing.

There is murmuring. The electricity of an urgent task.

He walks down the aisle and assigns you to a group: you are with the two American women in their sixties who boarded the bus after you.

You're about to stand when it occurs to you that you don't know what the missing person looks like. You say this to the women who are to be your partners.

"You're absolutely right," says the woman sitting closer

to you. "We haven't even been told who to look for." She laughs. "It's not a funny situation, someone being lost in that labyrinth, but it's very funny that this entire bus is about to go looking for someone without even knowing a description!

"Excuse me," she calls out to the tour guide. "Who are we looking for exactly? I mean, besides a missing person?"

The tour guide's face tightens with momentary panic. "Who do you think is missing?" he says. "You were all sitting here."

It's suddenly clear to everyone: The tour guide doesn't know who you're looking for. He has no name or physical description.

Everyone starts talking at once. The majority of people think it is a woman who's missing. They remember seeing a woman. "I think she was of Oriental descent," calls out one woman.

"You mean she was Asian?" says a Japanese American man toward the front.

"Yes," says the woman. "That's what I meant."

"I would have noticed if there was another Asian tourist on this bus," the Japanese man says.

"I think she was in her forties," says a stout grandmother. "Sort of nondescript."

"That's your description of our missing passenger?" says one of the shrinking husbands. "That she's nondescript! God help us."

"I mean that I think her hair was of average length and of average color," says the stout grandmother, clearly embarrassed.

"I can almost picture her," a woman in front of you says.

"How do you picture her?" says a male passenger behind you.

"I said I could almost picture her," says the woman in front of you.

"Well," says the man behind you. "When you can more completely picture her, please let us know."

The tour guide is nervous.

"Let's start looking for someone who looks lost," he says unhelpfully. "I think there's a good chance she will recognize one of you. She will come to you looking for help. I will carry my umbrella so she can come to me. I'm sure she will recognize the umbrella. People who want to stay on the bus can stay. Hassan, our driver, will be here. He will keep the doors closed and the air-conditioning on. He will call me if our missing passenger returns."

"But how will *we* know to come back to the bus if you've found her?" says a husband who looks less shrunken than the others. "I don't know about the rest of you, but my cell phone doesn't work here."

The tour guide ponders the question.

"We will all meet back here at the bus in one and a half hours," he says. "It is almost one thirty now. We will meet back here at three o'clock. Please stay with your partners. Please make note of each turn you take. We can't have any more missing people."

The searchers leave the bus, and the tour guide instructs everyone that to cover more territory, each group should travel in a different direction. He opens up his umbrella. "I'm going this way," he says, pointing left. An older couple accompanies him.

You follow your partners—Samantha and Hazel—to the right. Samantha is tall and round, with short brown hair streaked with blond highlights. She's the one you thought you might recognize, but she's wearing the Converses with zippers. Hazel is short and petite, with long stick-straight hair; she's wearing gold sandals.

"What's your name?" Hazel asks you.

"Jane," you say.

Hazel has a yellow fanny pack, which she wears on her belly. "It's her belly pack," Samantha teases. Hazel unzips it and removes a medium-size notebook and a thin green pen.

"I'm going to write down each turn we take," she says.

"Good idea," Samantha says.

Hazel looks around for a landmark. There's a sign above you that's written in Arabic and the three of you agree it won't help you unless Hazel copies down each letter exactly, and even then, it might not be of use.

"That looks like a hair salon," Samantha says, pointing to a barbershop.

"That's a good landmark," Hazel says.

You consider saying something about how many hair salons there are, and how it won't help. Hazel begins sketching the salon. You wonder how much territory the three of you will cover if she illustrates every landmark at every turn.

You watch the quick strokes she makes with the pen. She's good. The rendering is convincing. The pen is a souvenir; on its side it says *The Louvre*.

"Okay, all set," Hazel says after a few minutes. Together you walk another dozen feet until you come to a fork.

"Right or left?" you say.

"Up to you," Samantha says.

You turn right and Hazel pauses to illustrate a complicated handle on a squat door. The handle is silver and has an animal engraved on it.

After a minute you continue walking. You pass by a chamber with a fountain inside.

"What's this?" Samantha says, peering in.

"I don't know, but let's go in for a second. I'm hot out there. Are you hot, Jane?"

It takes you a moment to realize she's talking to you. Your name is not Jane.

"It *is* getting hot out," you say. "I think my ears might even be sweating."

"Your ears!" Samantha says, pausing to feel her own. "That's funny."

You all step inside the room with the fountain. The tile on the floor is turquoise and baby blue, cracked. Along the walls dozens of notices—all in Arabic—have been thumbtacked. Is it a center of worship? You see no sign or symbolism that it's a place of prayer. You have no idea why the room is open to the public.

The tiled floor must have recently been mopped because there's a strong scent of bleach. Hazel sits on the bench and starts sketching again.

"Much better in here with the tiles and the water," Samantha says, and extends a hand to feel the fountain water. "Are your ears still sweating, Jane?"

You make a show of touching them, checking them. "Nope, all good." You touch the water, too. It's not as cold as you expected. Its flow curls around your fingers, your palm. You dry your hand on your jeans.

You sit down on the bench next to Hazel. Samantha sits on the other side of her. Hazel starts sketching while looking at you. You turn away.

"Look this way," Hazel says. "Don't be shy."

You turn back to her. "You realize I'm not a landmark, right?"

"So where are you from?" Hazel asks, still sketching.

"Florida," you say.

"Oh, Samantha here is from Florida," Hazel says.

"Really," you say. "Miami?"

"No, the Gulf Coast," Samantha says. "Near Sarasota. A town called Dellis Beach."

You are from Dellis Beach.

"Where are *you* from?" they ask, almost in unison.

You try to not to pause. You need to say a place in Florida that's not Dellis Beach.

"Miami," you say.

"Oh, because I was going to say you look familiar," Samantha says. She looks at you, tilts her head back, taking you in.

Your mind moves quickly, miraculously. "I think you might have been on my flight to Casablanca. On the nineteenth?" you say. "You probably saw me there."

"I *was* on that flight," Samantha says. "Isn't that a coincidence? That must be where I recognize you from." She pauses as though remembering something. You're afraid of what she's going to say. "Did you see that woman who kept having to get her suitcase down from the overhead compartment?" she asks.

"Yeah," you say, and laugh.

Samantha turns to Hazel. "There was this woman sitting on my side of the plane in this crazy patterned dress who kept taking her suitcase down, opening it, and then putting it up and taking it down, opening it, and putting it up. She must have done it a hundred times."

"At least," you say.

Samantha studies Hazel's sketch. "That's so good, Hazy," she says. She stares at it a moment more, then turns to you. "You just look so familiar," she says to you. "Further back than the plane. If only my mind still worked the way it did when we were in college."

"The hazards of age," Hazel says. "But there are some things I'm glad not to remember."

"Like what?" Samantha says. "You're the least regretful person I know."

Hazel seems about to offer an example of something she's glad to have forgotten. "You know what?" she says. "I can't think of anything."

"See, told you," Samantha says. They both laugh.

"You went to college together?" you say.

"Yes, Florida State University," Samantha says.

"So you were with the big group of women on the plane? What happened to them?"

"Oh, we all went to Marrakech together, but then when we went to Casablanca, the rest of the ladies wanted to spend a few days there. Our guidebook said that when you get to Casablanca, the first thing you should do is get out of Casablanca. So we did."

Samantha stares at the sketch Hazel is making of you. She takes out a pair of glasses from her pack, and puts them on, and that's when you know for certain that it's her. She looks exactly as she did that day.

"You know who you look like?" Samantha says to you, then turns to Hazel. "Your drawing makes her look like that woman I was telling you about, that one in the delivery room. Remember how I was telling you I didn't know which twin to give the baby to?"

"Oh, you have to tell her that story," Hazel says to Samantha.

You know the story. The story is about you. You are not ready. You don't ever want to hear this story.

"I don't know if you know anything about Dellis Beach but it's pretty small—around twenty thousand people—and near Sarasota," Samantha says. "There's a young community and an old community."

You need to get away from these women, from this story.

"Which community are you part of, Sam?" Hazel asks.

"Ha!" Samantha says. "I will remind you that even though I graduated a year ahead of you at FSU, we are technically only seven months apart."

"So were you roommates?" you say. You hope this question will change the conversation, that it will unleash a tidal wave of memories of their college days.

"No," they both say at the same time.

You try not to let your disappointment show. You need the subject to change.

"Anyway," Samantha says, "back to my story. There were these two young couples in town. The girls were twin sisters. They were really close, but one was prettier than the other."

"Is that relevant?" Hazel says. "You're so lookist sometimes."

"I'm lookist? Don't be calling me any kind of 'ist.' I am as fair as they come."

"Right," says Hazel. She winks at you.

"Saw that," Samantha says. "So there were two equally beautiful twin sisters in our town," she continues, smiling.

"Were they identical or fraternal . . . or do you call them sororal?" Hazel asks.

"I think they were fraternal," Samantha says.

You shift closer to the edge of the bench, wondering if you could make it out the doorway fast enough to avoid being followed. Samantha will recognize you soon.

"So tell her what happens," Hazel says. "I'm almost done here, by the way. Sorry to keep you ladies captive but I'm really excited about this drawing."

"No problem," Samantha says, turning back to you, eyes alight. "So this was about two months ago now. I was the nurse on duty at my hospital and this one twin gives birth—it's an intense birth, no pain medication. She insisted on doing it natural, if you can imagine. She gives birth to this beautiful girl, a nose like Cleopatra's."

You wince. You stare out the doorway of the room. You have to get away.

"I think I see her," you say.

"Who?" Hazel says.

"The missing woman. I saw her pass by. I'm going to go ahead if you don't mind."

"Go! Find her!" Samantha says. "We'll catch up."

You walk quickly out of the room, and then when you're out of their sight, you run. You hear your breath. As you round a corner, you collide with pedestrians and apologize without stopping. You turn to see if Hazel and Samantha are behind you. You think you see them. You duck under a stairwell to hide. Someone's coming down the stairs. You keep moving. You picture your sister. You picture the baby. You remember how the nurse, whose name you now know is Samantha, held her out to you, but your sister intercepted. She took the baby from Samantha, and rocked her uncomfortably.

You pulled the sheet of the bed up and over your head and covered your face. You stayed like that until Samantha gently pulled the sheet down to your shoulders. "Oh, honey," she said. "This isn't a morgue."

You run down a narrow passageway with small doors. Laundry hangs above you. You hear a baby crying, you hear someone playing an oud. You smell urine.

Friends who had given birth themselves had warned you about the third day after birth, how the hormones would overtake your body and you would be left a sobbing mess.

You didn't think it would happen to you. You thought your experience would be different because the baby was not your own. But it was worse.

You run faster, harder.

Your sister came to your house, a week after the birth. She rang your doorbell. She never rang your doorbell. Usually she knocked or used the key. She knew where the key was hidden: underneath the paint can next to the recycling bin.

You opened the door. "What, no baby?" you said.

"She's with the nanny," she said.

You told her you'd love to help out whenever you could; you reminded her that you hadn't seen the baby as much as you expected.

"Can we sit?" she said as she stood on your doorstep.

"Of course," you said, and she entered and sat down at the kitchen table. You made tea for both of you. You feared that she was going to tell you the baby was sick, that she was dying. There was a somber tone to her arrival at your doorstep.

"I love you," she said.

"I love you too," you said. Your concern grew. You rarely told each other this. What was wrong with the baby?

"I don't want what I'm about to tell you to be personal," she said.

"Okay," you said, swallowing hard. You knew that meant it would be personal.

"Do you have something stronger than tea?" she said.

"Like coffee?" you said.

"No, like vodka."

You made your sister a vodka tonic. "I have fresh limes from my neighbor's garden," you said to fill the silence.

"It's fine as is," she said.

You placed the drink in front of her.

"I've been disloyal," she said to you.

"Oh no," you said, thinking, *Thank God it's not about the baby.*

"For how long?" you said.

"Five months now."

"I'm sure things with the fertility . . . I'm sure everything got complicated," you said. "Maybe you and Drew can see a counselor."

"It did get complicated," she said.

You run through a tiny courtyard where boys are playing soccer. You almost trip over the ball. You keep running, and the boys' laughter follows you.

Your sister asked for another drink. You made her one. This time you placed a slice of the lime on the rim.

"Who's the man?" you said.

"That's what I came to talk to you about."

She paced. She walked out to the deck, and then back again.

"I can't do this," she said.

"Can't do what?" you said.

"It's him," she said. You followed her gaze. She was looking at your husband's socks. He was in the habit of taking them off when he was reading on the couch and leaving them on the floor.

"Who?" you said.

She didn't answer.

"Who?" you said, this time louder.

"I'm so sorry," she said, looking at the socks.

You run faster. You can hear your heartbeat pounding in your ears. Your sandals slap against the cobblestone.

Your husband didn't come home that night, or the next. You left him messages on his cell phone telling him not to bother. But you hoped he would bother, you hoped he would care. You imagined him coming in the front door and finding you wherever you were in the house and telling you your sister had a problem: she'd entwined your lives so thoroughly that she'd gotten herself confused. But he didn't call, and didn't return to the home you no longer wanted to live in.

You called your husband's parents. You wanted them to know, but the conversation had exploded into accusations and lies and screaming. You called Drew, your sister's husband, and he told you your sister and your husband were planning on living together with the baby. He told you he was suing his wife, and your husband, for custody. This conversation too ended loudly, and you hung up, threw the phone, broke the phone. Broke everything of your husband's, told him not to come back for anything—it was all broken, burned, sold.

Your nipples still ached. Your milk had come in and you had not nursed. You called the midwife and told her your breasts felt they were being pricked by pins. She advised you to buy cabbage leaves and keep them in your freezer, and to periodically place one of them on your nipples. You lay on the floor of your bedroom with cold cabbage leaves cupping your breasts.

You tried to avoid mirrors. Your body was still swollen, the veins on your chest and legs a sickly blue. You called your boss and quit. He had refused to give you maternity leave. He had said to you: "It's not like you're really a mother, now is it?"

A week after your sister had come to your house, the midwife knocked on the door. "You didn't answer my calls," she said when you looked out the peephole. You told her everything. She held you tight, and then helped you put all your things in storage. You stayed at her house, slept on her couch under a blanket she had knitted for a baby she had lost in the final trimester. She told you about Morocco; she'd lived there after college, had traveled alone and met new friends, one of them a midwife. She made you want to go, go to the desert, see new things, to experience what it was like to be a woman in a country like that. She told you it would give you a new perspective, which you hoped, at the time, meant that you would see everything as a mirage.

Your breath is hot and loud. You reach an empty, residential square, and rest with your back against the wall of a small terra-cotta house. Soon your breath is even, almost calm. It's this calm that has surprised you before. You panic and you rage, then this calm settles over you, and you remake yourself.

A vendor wearing Versace sunglasses that are fake or stolen approaches you. You don't know how he's found you here and you wish he'd go away.

"Hello, lady," he says. "Hello, nice lady."

He is in his early twenties. "I have camera you like. Nice camera."

"No, thank you," you say.

"Pretty lady like you, you should take photographs of you. Here, I take photograph of you."

"No," you say. "Please don't. Please leave me alone."

He looks to his left, then to his right before pulling out the camera. It's a Pentax, not so different from the one you owned. But this one has a bigger lens and looks more expensive.

You do not want a camera, but you want him to go away.

"How much?" you say.

"For you, lady, three hundred and sixty dirhams."

"Excuse me?" you say. If you're doing your math right, it's only forty dollars.

"Okay. Two hundred and sixty dirhams." Thirty dollars.

"Okay," you say. You need him to go away.

You turn from him, and extract the money from your bra. You make the exchange quickly, and he is gone, and you are once again alone in the small square.

You hold the camera in your hands—it's heavy, a professional's camera. You turn it on. The first few photos are of a woman with strawberry-blond hair. She's in a Moroccan city—Fez? She's in her late thirties, with soft wrinkles around her eyes when she smiles, which she does a lot—it's a natural, unforced smile. In most of the photos she wears loose pants and a tight T-shirt. Her clothes don't look American—maybe she's Dutch, or Danish. You continue rewinding. Now she's standing in front of what looks like a Gaudí balcony in Barcelona. Her arms are outstretched, as though to say, *Look where I am!*

In many of the photos she's posing with her son. Her son is skinny and tall, and partial to wearing the same soccer shirt every day. He's about eleven, you guess, with freckles scattered just below his blue eyes. You flip through more photos of this woman's life. You don't see a father or husband; it's just a mother and son on a trip. In one photo, they're both eating bright green ice cream from cones and the woman is laughing and licking her wrist—the ice cream melted and she's cleaning it off. In another, her son is posing in a museum, in front of a painting of a mournful-looking boy. The son is imitating the serious look of the boy in the painting, but the son can't contain himself—you see a smile emerging.

You scroll through hundreds of photos, until you're back to the first. In this inital photo, the woman and her son are at a European airport, their luggage beside them on the curb. The boy is standing in front of his mother, and her hands are placed casually on his shoulders. You zoom in. The gesture is protective but not possessive.

Something about these photographs, and this one in particular, gives you a sense of peace. You feel the familiar blue wave of calm take you over.

"That's a good one," a voice behind you says.

You jump.

"So sorry," says the man. He's in his early forties, with graying blond hair, and speaks with an accent you can't place.

"I didn't mean to surprise you. I just wonder if you're a photographer."

He's wearing a heavy Nikon camera on a strap around his
neck. He's thin and tall, his hair a little long but still respect-
ably cut. You're angry with him for approaching you like that,
for getting so close. People don't do that here in Morocco. He
should know this.

"Are you a professional?" he asks, looking at your camera.

"I just bought it," you say.

"You should put a strap on it," he says. "Or keep it hidden.
I'm traveling with a bunch of journalists and photographers,
and one of them had their camera stolen the other day."

You're suddenly interested. "You're with the press pool?"

"Yes," he says, surprised you know.

"I saw your vans park beside our bus. What are you covering exactly?"

"We've been going all over North Africa with this Nige-
rian politician. Kind of fun. Most of us are bloggers, a random
bunch from all over—I'm from Zurich. Some of us are pros,
others amateurs . . . it doesn't seem to matter. We basically
just document what he says and does. Show him being interested in local problems, being kind to poor people, that sort of
thing. Turns out to be a very lovely man, so it makes the job
easy."

A car horn turns the Swiss man's head.

"I should go," he says. "I'm supposed to be back in the van
soon. Lovely to meet you."

But you haven't introduced yourselves.

You stand in the middle of the small square, thinking

about your options. There are ways out of your predicament. You can't go back to the bus. And you can't go to the embassy in Casablanca where Susan Sontag works, but there must be another embassy. Maybe in Rabat. You continue walking, and the streets grow gradually busier and more crowded. Eventually you spot a courtyard ahead of you. You walk toward it, hoping there's a taxi stand.

When you emerge into the large plaza, the sun, which has been shielded from you by the narrow walkways, assaults you again. You're momentarily blinded.

"There she is!" says a voice.

You look up. You see Hazel, Samantha, and the tour guide walking toward you.

"It was *you*," Samantha says.

"What?" you say.

"It was you all along," says Hazel.

You scan your options. You can lie.

"You were the missing person we were looking for," says the tour guide. He is angry but is trying to appear relieved.

The missing person. That's who they think you are? So they don't know that you're the woman from Dellis Beach?

"I found a wig," the tour guide says. "You must have changed seats . . . I must have counted you twice, and you must have paid twice, once on each side of the bus! I didn't realize you were someone else."

"You're the person you've been looking for!" Samantha says. "Isn't that hilarious?"

You don't answer. You hold the camera firmly.

The tour guide turns to Samantha. "It's not so funny,"

he says. "The police are at the bus. The tour company called them an hour ago when they thought we had an actual missing person."

He looks at you accusingly.

"I had no idea," you say. "I really didn't. I'm sorry."

"We just have to explain it to them and sign a few forms," the tour guide says. "Then we go back to Casablanca." The nuisance of it all appears to exhaust him. He looks like he's frustrated that he studied history in school and now his job is counting people's heads on buses. "Let's go," he says.

"I just need to use the bathroom," you say.

You go into the bathroom of a café in the plaza and lock the door. You take a paper towel and run it under cool water, and press the towel to your forehead. You don't want to face the stares of all the passengers on the bus, who will surely be angry that they spent hours of the tour looking for you. And worse: The police will ask for your name. They will ask for ID. They will want to know who you are.

You stare at your colorful basket, at the clothes you purchased for your mother this morning. You take off your white blouse and your black jeans and pull on the beaded blue and white djellaba. You remove your sandals and slip on the pointed orange babouche.

This is how you pictured yourself in Morocco. Not at a police station, not on a film set, but as a woman dressed to blend in while seeing North Africa for the first time. You pull the hood of the djellaba over your head.

You place the clothes you were wearing in the basket and throw it out the small window of the bathroom. You know the basket will be found in minutes, that someone will sell the clothes and sandals, or wear them.

You exit the bathroom. You see the tour guide, Hazel, and Samantha talking. You avoid them, walk far enough away from them that they don't recognize you. You're covered, you're wearing different clothes. You imagine that from a distance you look like a Moroccan.

You approach the parking lot and see the police waiting by your tour bus. In front of the bus are three vans—the ones belonging to the press pool. You see the Swiss man boarding the middle van. Holding your camera in front of you, you get on after him. The driver turns to look at you. "She was in the other van," the Swisss man says. "I think she enjoyed shopping the souks!" The driver nods. The Swiss man smiles at you, gently, as though to imply *Don't worry, you owe me nothing*. And you believe him.

The other passengers in the van barely turn to look at you. They are busy discussing what they had for lunch. You overhear mention about the next day's flight from Rabat to Cairo. You sit quietly in your seat, listening to how loud your heart is beating, as you wait for it to slow down, to adapt.

The van doors close and the driver starts the engine. You pass by the tour bus, and the police, who are standing outside the bus, waiting for the missing woman who's been found. They are waiting for you.

As the van begins its drive out of Meknes, you see an intricate keyhole-shaped arch that leads into the ruins of what was once the royal palace. The arch is decorated with glazed blue, green, and red earthenware mosaics in the form of stars and rosettes. You watch as one woman enters through the arch, and another exits. You snap a photo, the first one of many you will take with this new camera, someone else's camera.

Now that you are past the tour bus and the police, your heartbeat has adjusted and normalized. You look down at your outfit—your blue and white djellaba, your orange slippers. You never dress so brightly. You think of the redheaded bodyguard and how he spoke of that blue and orange species of bird and its radical evolution. Was that what he'd called it? You pull off the hood of your blue djellaba. Out the window, you see wide fields of sunflowers, their golden-yellow heads rising up like periscopes above an ocean of green.

A Spanish woman in the passenger seat of the van, whose name you've made out to be Paloma, is searching for a good song on the radio. She gives up and inserts a CD and you hear:

> *Looking out on the morning rain*
> *I used to feel so uninspired*
> *And when I knew I had to face another day*
> *Lord, it made me feel so tired*

When the chorus comes on she promptly turns it off and the women in the van go mute and listen to all the men belt out "You make me feel like a natural woman." Paloma turns around and gives you, the closest woman to where she's sitting, a wide smile. You laugh.

The Swiss man laughs too, even though he was singing the lyrics the loudest. He turns toward you. The afternoon sun is flooding the van with golden light now, and he shields his eyes to see you. "I don't think we were really properly introduced," he says.

You look at him—his eyes have a flash of lavender in them. Others on the van are now waiting for your name too. For a moment you consider giving them your real name, but you're not ready. So you think of beautiful names—Verity, Maya, Honorée. No, no. You'll save those for when you have a daughter of your own. For now, you look into the sun and you smile. "It's funny this song is playing," you tell them. "My name is actually Aretha."

out the immeasurable gift of time. As always, I am forever indebted to those who have allowed for those elusive and essential hours and days: my parents, Paul and Inger, my sister, Vanessa and her family, my own young children, and, especially, Dave.

ACKNOWLEDGMENTS

Thank you to my editor and publisher, Dan Halpern, and to Gabriella Doob, Allison Saltzman, Craig Young, Sonya Cheuse, Ashley Garland, Stephanie Vallejo, Martin Karlow, Stephanie Mendoza, Bridget Read, and everyone else at Ecco. Thank you to Karen Duffy and everyone at Atlantic Books, and to Iris Tupholme at HarperCollins Canada.

Thank you to Mary Evans, and to Julia Kardon and Mary Guale at Mary Evans, Inc., and to Felicity Rubenstein at Lutyens & Rubinstein, and Lindsay Williams at the Gotham Group.

I'm grateful to Adrian Tomine, for the beautiful cover, and to early readers of this manuscript for their edits and insights: Heidi Julavits, Sheila Heti, Sarah Stewart Taylor, Lisa Michaels, Sarah Stone, Ann Packer, Ron Nyren, Cornelia Nixon, Ann Cummins, Clara Sankey, and Em-J Staples.

Thank you to Andi Winnette, Andrew Leland, Ross Simonini, Karolina Waclawiak, Dominic Luxford, and everyone at *The Believer* magazine.

A book cannot be written, let alone conceived of, with-